KENZO

KENZO

KIMBERLEY YOUNG

Printed in the United Kingdom

First Printing: Mar 2023

ISBN-978-1-7392465-2-5

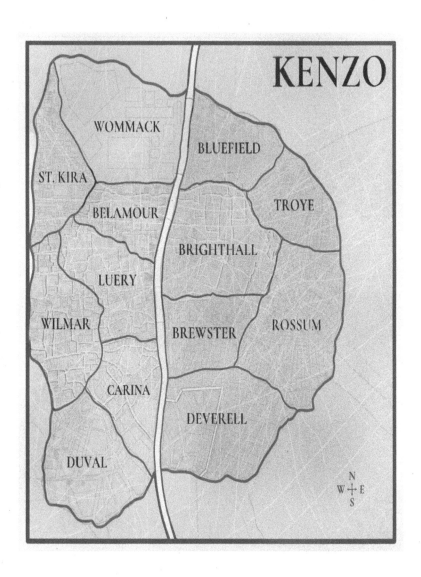

CHAPTER 1

February 23rd 1995

Sat alone at the back of a weather-beaten bus, Alexandria Raffaello shifted in her seat. She stared out of the window and through the mist, at the road rushing past. The burnt orange of the setting sun bled into the darkening sky overhead as the bus rattled its way into the boundaries of Kenzo.

The heat from the engine below Alex's seat had risen to fill the entire back row and thickened the air surrounding her. It clung to her skin and hair and fogged the windows around her.

She tugged at the collar of her t-shirt, fidgeting as the cotton stuck to her sweaty back and she huffed in irritation. The seat she was sitting on was a fire pit.

Her eyes fell on her backpack on the seat next to her. She grabbed the handle and dragged it to rest on her lap.

The clunky bag rattled as it settled and groaned as she unzipped it. She shoved her hand in the mouth and felt around until she found the crumpled newspaper she had gotten from Oakland's bus station.

The pages fluttered as she fanned herself with it, but there was barely any relief from the stale air smothering her and with the bag now on her lap, she only became more irritated.

Initially, she had welcomed the warmth after hours in the cold, but hours in the boiling heat had been just as unwelcome.

After reading through the newspaper three times over the duration of her journey, there was not a single article that she hadn't read, but still, she flipped through it once more before she decided to shove it back down in her bag. With a sigh, she slumped over in her seat and returned to staring out of the window.

The bus had been late leaving the station back in Oakland by over an hour and a half. Alex had then spent two hours after that trapped on the bus, as the overheated metal box on wheels made its way from Oakland to Kenzo with a handful of people. The other passengers had all chosen to sit up front, leaving Alex alone at the back to fight off the heat and boredom.

The bus turned off from the main road and onto a quieter and narrower road, where dense, wild foliage sprang up on both sides. It enclosed them in the cool shadow of the trees and hid the bus from the warmth of the sunset.

Alex's foot drummed an erratic beat against the floor, as she played with the frayed handles of her bag. Her eyes had glazed over as she stared ahead, watching out of the windshield as the road coiled to the left. It carved its way through the surrounding trees and the rising mist, while the evening sky darkened around them.

As the bus lurched its way around the bends in the road, Alex glanced down at her tattered watch. The glass had fractured, and the black strap had peeled in places, but it ticked on steadily.

According to her watch, it was now a quarter past six. Alex's nostrils flared, and she slumped further back in her seat as the engine continued to rumble beneath her.

The bus should have arrived at the next bus stop by now. According to the timetable stuck to the bulletin board at the station, the bus Alex needed to get next was due to arrive in ten minutes. If she missed this one, she would have to wait for at least another hour. It would leave her completely stranded until another bus arrived.

After another twenty minutes of driving along what felt like the same stretch of road on a loop, the road forked in two. On the right, the road curved around a mass of trees and then out of sight. On the left, the road ended at the mouth of a large shelter. Inside the building were dozens of buses identical to the one she was on, lined up neatly inside.

At the sight, Alex sprang out of her seat, pressing her face to the glass for a better look.

As Kenzo's bus garage emerged from the darkening gloom, she grabbed the straps of her backpack and swung it onto her back. It collided with her spine with a muffled smack, almost knocking the air from her lungs. The dull pain bloomed from the spot, but she ignored it as she checked her seat before she stumbled into the aisle.

She stretched her legs as she walked, trying to get some feeling back into them that hours of sitting in one spot had taken away. The bus lurched to a creaking stop in front of the garage, sinking to the ground with a groan.

The bus driver announced their arrival and opened the doors to the few people on board.

The other passengers got up and left the bus ahead of her as soon as the doors opened. They cast long inky shadows in the evening light as they dispersed into the oncoming dark.

Alex was the last to leave the bus. As she stepped out into the cold evening and her feet touched the tarmac, the crisp winter chill engulfed her, bursting into the stifling bubble of warm air surrounding her. She inhaled through her nose greedily, filling her lungs slowly as she savoured it, even as she tried not to sneeze from the temperature change.

The bus closed its doors behind her and drove further into the gigantic bus garage, joining the other buses inside.

Alex adjusted her backpack and pulled out the crumpled paper she called her map from inside her coat pocket.

Yesterday, she had spent at least half an hour in Oakland's Public Library, copying the directions from the computer. The library printer had been broken, so she used her pen and a sheet from her notebook to write out the directions and drew the map by hand. The map itself wouldn't have been much help without the written directions to guide her, but it helped her to know which direction she should head and which road to take.

According to her map, the next bus stop she needed was near. A stone's throw away if she had drawn it properly.

She oriented herself as she lined up the surrounding landmarks with the ones on the map before setting off in the right direction.

The road she walked along was lonely and lined with thick patches of trees on both sides. With every minute that passed, the sky darkened even more, drawing out shadows that clutched at Alex as she ambled by.

The winter air rustled through the leaves, following so closely behind her it brushed against her legs, but Alex paid the wind no attention.

She could feel the minutes slipping by, as the evening blurred into the night but, there was nothing to be done about that, except to keep going.

Just one more bus and she would be in Troye.

She followed the road back from where the bus had come. It led her away from the bus garage, back to where it had split into two, and she continued walking along the road as it led to the right, towards the next bus stop.

As she walked, the pavement became increasingly narrow where the woods outgrew their boundaries, until Alex had to hop over branches that stretched out into her path to trip her.

After a few more minutes of walking, a rusted metallic glint caught her eye.

The bus stop was derelict. The foliage that had overgrown the woodlands almost hid the bus stop from view as it attempted to smother the landmark. It stood underneath a rusting lamppost that was still unlit, despite the hour. Rust had also covered the shelter, and the bench was scratched and worn. Old wrappers and scraps of paper were the only sign that anyone had been here recently, but Alex didn't care. She was just happy to have found it. It was the only bus stop near enough that would get her anywhere near Troye. All the rest avoided it. This was the most direct route.

With a yawn, she swung her backpack off one shoulder and settled down onto the metal bench as it gave a concerning creak. She checked her watch again. Twenty-five minutes past six.

She tried to relax, or at least, to settle into her seat, but she couldn't. Every movement she made, she took care to not put too much weight on it, since the bench and the shelter groaned in agony every time she moved. The last thing she wanted was for the whole thing to collapse on top of her. She chuckled darkly at the thought as she pictured both her legs sticking out from under a pile of rusted scrap metal.

Despite the delay, she was on time. No bus had passed her on the way there, so she hoped that was a sign that she was back on track. She folded her hands and began her patient vigil for her bus.

To Troye, and then she would be at *Cassandra's Palace*.

Ten minutes later, Alex had lost a lot of her optimism, along with her body heat.

She prised herself from the frozen seat with a sniffle and began pacing around with her icy hands buried in her pockets. To pass the time, she made a note of everything she saw, and when she had finished with that, she started all over again.

Over an hour later, Alex was still waiting, though not as patiently.

Ice-cold air swirled around Alex as she shivered beside the battered bus stop. She scowled up at the unlit lamp post and wiped her nose on the arm of her coat as she returned to naming her surroundings for what felt like the thousandth time that evening.

The wind whistled around her, dragging the scraps of trash around the pavement. Now, in the gloom of nightfall, they disappeared out of sight only a few feet away.

Alex rubbed her eyes and took out the map again. Her eyes skimmed over the information as she reread what she had written.

She was currently in Rossum, just inside the boundaries of Kenzo. When the bus arrived, it would take her to another bus stop inside Troye, and from there, she'd walk to *Cassandra's Palace*. She knew this already, but she had hoped that there had been something she had missed or misread. Something that would at least help to ease the worry rolling around in the pit of her stomach.

Maybe she had the information wrong. Was she at the wrong bus stop?

Alex's eyes skimmed over the paper once more and, after finding nothing new to help her situation, she scrunched up the paper and shoved it back into her pocket.

Again, she looked at her watch. The time was now a quarter to eight.

Alex shifted the backpack on her back, hissing in pain as the weight of it moved along her spine and pulled at her sore shoulders. Staring ahead, she frowned at the empty road in front of her as she recalled the last eight hours.

She had woken up early, left at a decent time in the morning, and had even taken the time to plan out her journey days before. But, no matter how much she thought about it, Alex couldn't see where she could have done anything differently to prevent this from happening.

Alex shivered again as the hair on the back of her neck stood up. An icy chill, separate from the wind swirling around her, ran throughout the length of her body. The feeling that she was no longer alone almost suffocated her as she felt the heavy weight of a presence watching her. It settled around her neck and pulled her shoulders down. Her breathing became shallow, and she tried to listen above the pounding heartbeat in her ears.

After a weighted pause, the heavy silence that had coated the air broke with a crisp snap.

Every muscle in Alex's body froze at the sound, coiled and waiting to be used as the noise dragged her attention back to her present situation.

The sound was sharp. Heavy. Deliberate. A sound caused by the intentional movement of something living and not just wind rustling through the trees.

Directly opposite Alex was another massive wooded area that ran alongside the road. She had only given it a cursory glance during the last few minutes that the sun had been out while she had waited. But now that it was dark, the menacing, dense trees pulled most of her attention.

The loss of the pale sun had caused the opaque black shadows of the trees to cover most of the ground. They reached toward Alex like long, spindly hands.

She squinted at the trees, but they were so dark and tightly packed together that she could barely see the individual branches. To Alex, it was all a dense wall of inky darkness.

That was where the sound had come from.

Staring at the trees, Alex realised that her mouth had dropped open to let in the short, shallow breaths attempting to fill her lungs. She closed it and inhaled deeply through her nose.

She focused on keeping the rest of her breaths slow, deep and almost silent as she strained her ears for more sounds. Her dark eyes skimmed over the tree trunks again, looking for any movement.

She was in the middle of nowhere. And completely stranded. She could barely see a few feet in front of her. The area was unfamiliar. Moving from her spot would cause her to get lost in the woods. The cold had seized her muscles and her movements had become sluggish.

Whoever or whatever was out there had a clear advantage. She wouldn't be able to outrun them or hide.

Slowly, she reached into her coat pocket and closed her fingers around the cold metal canister she kept in grabbing distance.

She waited.

After a few seconds passed by with no further movement, she began to question if the noise had been a hallucination of her tired mind or not.

The shadows and her lack of sleep might have tricked her survival instincts into thinking she was in danger.

Fear and lack of sleep had fuelled her imagination.

She had almost convinced herself that this was what had happened.

Exhaustion overcame her for a split second, and her eyes closed. When she opened them again, she noticed a change in her surroundings. Seconds before, she had been staring ahead into the pitch-black shadows that coated the trees.

Now, in the pit, there was a pair of eyes staring out at her.

Glowing softly, almost like golden beacons, two pinpricks of light emerged from the dark. They were directly ahead of Alex, on the opposite side of the road, nestled between branches and smaller twigs.

She knew the lights in front of her were eyes because while there was no sign that the owner was blinking, the two small orbs of yellow light moved together. No matter how they shifted, the lights remained the same distance apart.

There was an intensity behind the light, the same weighted feeling she had felt before she saw them.

There was something in the dark watching her.

The light beckoned her closer, but her feet remained anchored where she was.

They swayed softly, weaving from right to left, as if whatever owned them was shifting its weight experimentally, considering her where she stood frozen.

The lights tilted to the right again and paused for a moment.

That was when the mass of smaller branches framing the lights shifted.

Alex pulled back sharply, trying to put more distance between her and whatever was across the road. The sound of rustling and snapping twigs filled the air as the figure watching her moved closer to her. Alex dropped the tiny can of pepper spray back into her pocket as her heart raced.

She would need an actual weapon. She would have to fight.

But would she have enough time to get to her backpack to search for one?

As she grabbed the strap of her bag, a heavy rumble broke the air and stole her attention. Before her observer could breach the dense wall of trees, the bright headlights of a truck sliced through the dark road between them as it roared over the hill and into view.

While the incoming vehicle was not her bus, she preferred her chances with the hood of the truck over whatever was waiting for her across the road.

She stepped out into the road, in the path of the truck, waving her arms above her head to catch the driver's attention and the bright headlights of the truck bathed her in light.

The rustling in the trees faded as it fled in the opposite direction and the sound of its retreat drowned underneath the bellowing engine. The driver acknowledged her with a flash of the headlights as it slowed.

The truck's roar overwhelmed her senses, just as its bulky frame rolled to a stop directly in front of her and the interior cab light switched on.

CHAPTER 2

The truck that had come to Alex's rescue was large and sturdy. That was the first thing she noticed. The navy blue paint had chips in some areas and thick mud caked along the tyres and bottom. When the cab light switched on, it illuminated both its driver and passenger.

His dark brows were angled down, making his scowl more prominent on his face as his eyes slid over her. The driver was a bear of a man with raven black hair that curled around his ears and down his neck. Grey strands weaved through his hair and the heavy stubble that covered his tanned face.

His nose was sharp and pointed, and underneath his stubble, his jaw was wide and square. He wore a dark green shirt that made his piercing, hazel eyes lean towards green. The dark brown leather jacket he wore was well-loved, and his jeans had faded with time.

Even as he sat, he looked huge, at least over six feet tall. His build was broad and sturdy, just like the truck he drove.

Next to him in the passenger seat was another man, a few years younger than him. His face was just as tanned, only rounder. His hair was just as dark, but without the tint of grey. Unlike the man next to him, he was clean-shaven, and he had recently trimmed his hair. But just like his companion, he wore jeans, a button-up shirt and a black leather jacket. His dark eyes glittered in the orange light bathing the interior as he surveyed her. There was a crease between his thin brows, but he looked more curious than suspicious.

Her eyes narrowed as they flitted between the two men and then back across the road. Their eyes followed her gaze to scan the area for whatever had captured her attention.

As far as she could tell, there was no sign that whatever was prowling around in the shadows of the trees had returned to finish what it had started.

Alex turned back to the men, who were still staring at her expectantly. The man in the driver's seat raised his eyebrows. "You okay, miss?"

Hesitantly, Alex pulled the corners of her mouth up into a polite smile. She inclined her head towards them. Now that she was out of immediate danger, she wasn't sure how to explain herself. She rubbed her sweaty palms against her jeans as she rocked forwards on her feet. "I'm sorry to bother you," she started, her nose wrinkling as her mind whirled, "but I've been waiting for a bus for ages and I haven't seen one pass."

The passenger grimaced in sympathy. "The road was closed down a couple of hours ago and the buses along this route were diverted."

The driver gave a curt nod in agreement. "Don't worry. We can drop you off." He tapped a button and the sound of the doors unlocking filled the air. "Get in." He growled.

Alex eyed the back door warily and shifted on her feet. Her hands flexed as her eyes flickered from him to the other man beside him and back again.

The driver's abruptness put her back on guard and the thought that she had escaped one dangerous situation only to end up in another had crossed her mind.

At her hesitance, the man in the driver's seat fished inside his jacket and pulled out a police badge. "Sorry. My name is Detective Henry Lovett, and this is my partner,

Detective David Li." He rumbled. "We were out patrolling the area. As he said, there was an incident on another road earlier today, and the buses along this route are being diverted."

A chill swept over Alex, raising goosebumps on her skin. If this incident caused two detectives to be called out, it must be something serious. Alex didn't know much about the police force, but she doubted that two detectives would be out on patrol for a minor incident.

Reflexively, her eyes drifted back towards the patch of trees opposite.

Did this incident have anything to do with what she had seen before?

She couldn't tell the detectives what she saw, she knew that. She didn't have words for what she had seen. How could she, when she wasn't sure what it was she had seen?

And even if she could wade through her fragmented memory of the encounter to understand it, she would, at the very least, have to omit details to make the whole thing sound halfway plausible to someone else.

The worst-case scenario would be that they didn't take her seriously and simply brushed off what she had seen as a vivid imagination.

But the best-case scenario would be that they would get out of their truck and investigate.

In either case, the two detectives would be the best people for the job.

"You getting in?" The driver nodded towards the back seat of the truck. "Don't worry," he repeated evenly, as his fingers drummed an irregular beat on the steering wheel, "we'll drop you off on a main road, or something."

At his words, his passenger began clearing the back seat of all the discarded items thrown there haphazardly.

The pile was made from various files, stacked on top of a small black briefcase, a brown package, and an empty fast food paper bag. The passenger shoved it all unceremoniously onto the seat behind the driver. Alex's eyes scanned the truck's interior as he worked, checking for any weapons or other warning signs hidden in the back. Fortunately, the only concerning things were the multiple wrappers from a place called *Freddie's Grill*, a recently finished cigar stub on the dashboard, and a large silver flask they had thrown onto the backseat. The thick smell of cigar smoke had already wafted out through the window to meet her where she stood.

When he had finished, the man in the passenger seat nodded to the seat behind him. He smiled at her crookedly and she smiled back.

To be honest, the two men were probably a bigger risk to their hearts than they were to her.

Still...

Alex eyed the seat, but she hesitated, and her eyes flicked once again towards the trees opposite her. She let out an exhausted sigh as she considered her next few words.

"While I was waiting for a bus," she began, "just before you showed up, I think... I saw... I think I saw someone watching me from over there." She pointed towards the woods on the other side of the road.

The men in the truck looked towards the woods, then at each other. At the driver's nod, both of them exited the truck, their focus already directed towards where she had pointed. Alex tensed where she stood, keeping both of them in her line of sight.

"Over here?" Detective Lovett asked, pointing into the thicket she had indicated. As she had suspected, he towered over her and his younger companion. He reached into his jacket and pulled out a torch and then a gun from his holster under his jacket. Cautiously, he turned and walked over to the area. His movements were methodical and fluid as if he had done this a thousand times before.

Alex kept her eyes on his back as Detective Lovett walked to the trees. Detective Li turned to her and ushered her back to the truck. He placed her between him and the truck as he watched his partner's back.

She opened her mouth to say something, maybe to ask a question, but nothing came out. She stared after Detective Lovett, armed with only a gun and a torch in hand, as she waited with Detective Li.

A few questions were circling her mind, but despite her efforts, she found it nearly impossible to articulate them. She wanted to suggest that he went with his partner, but that would leave her alone on the road with their truck.

So, Alex waited with Detective Li by the side of the road. They waited in silence for his partner to return from the inky shadows that enveloped the trees.

As the night air swirled around them, she shivered, but now she wasn't sure if that was only because of the cold.

Her mind felt sluggish as if it was working a few seconds too slow, but somehow, the world around her was moving even slower still.

She needed to know what he would find out there. Had she been face to face with something that was a threat to her life, or had it just been a harmless hallucination she had made up in the dark?

Detective Li looked down at her over his shoulder. "You okay?"

It took a moment to register the words that had left his mouth, but when she did, Alex nodded slowly.

His brows lowered in concern, and he shot her a reassuring smile. "Don't worry. He's got this." He gestured in the direction Detective Lovett had gone as the other man shone his torch through the bushes. "So, how long ago did you see this person?"

"Uhm...about a few seconds before the two of you arrived." She chewed her lip for a moment as a thought entered her mind. "Can I see your badge again?" She whispered. Detective Lovett had shown his badge, but she wanted to get a better look at it, to make sure it was genuine and belonged to them.

And wasn't just plucked from the corpse of a cop.

It might have been paranoia that made her ask, but stranger things had happened that night.

Detective Li nodded, and slowly, he pulled out his badge and held it up for her to inspect. Her eyes drifted over the details, but she didn't know what a real detective's badge looked like. Though, if she had to guess, she supposed it looked something like this.

"So, you're...homicide detectives, right?"

Detective Li nodded with another crooked smile. "Yeah, we are."

"So, you're investigating a homicide?"

Detective Li's smile tightened at the edges as his forehead creased even further. "We're investigating a potential homicide." He clarified. "Nothing's certain yet."

"Oh." Alex hummed thoughtfully as he put the badge away. As she turned over his words in her head, her eyes narrowed. "If the incident wasn't a homicide, then what was it?" Her eyes traced over his features, ready to catch a lie.

Detective Li thought for a second before he shrugged. "It looks like it was just an animal. But, it's better to be safe than sorry." He shoved his hands in his pockets and kicked at the tarmac below their feet. He looked around at the open space around them, at the lonely road, the cracked pavements and the looming trees surrounding them. "So," he chirped, "what's your name?"

She cleared her dry throat. "Alexandria Raffaello."

His eyes widened. "Are you Italian?"

Her nose scrunched in confusion at the unfamiliar word. "No." She mumbled, unsure of what he was asking her. If he thought her name indicated anything about her, he would be wrong, since it wasn't hers, to begin with.

Detective Li's eyes betrayed his confusion before he gave her another lopsided smile. "And how long have you been waiting?"

Alex wrapped her fingers around the straps of her bag and raised her eyes to the pitch-black sky. "More than a few hours."

Just as her mind was drawn back to the past few hours she had been stranded, the sound of trees rustling caught their attention and they both looked up as Detective Lovett sauntered out of the thick of trees to join them. "Didn't find anything, but I'll call it in. Get someone to come and check it out. It might be related to what happened higher up." He muttered to his partner.

"I thought that incident was an animal attack," Alex interjected. "A possible one."

The older detective's head snapped towards her. He looked down his nose at her and frowned. Slowly, his eyes flicked to his partner. Detective Li gave him an apologetic look before Detective Lovett returned his attention to Alex.

"A possible animal attack occurred higher up the road, but nothing can be ruled out yet until we investigate." He scratched the back of his head before he let his arms fall to his sides. "But, you did say someone was watching you out here, right? You saw someone."

Alex gave a stiff nod, as her eyes flickered to his empty hands, unsure that she should commit to that claim any more than she already had.

Detective Lovett shrugged his large shoulders. "Well then, maybe, it's possible that someone wandered over here from the other crime scene."

"Someone?" Alex looked around at the dense, dark forest that sprang up on both sides of the road they were on. "Why would anyone be out here?"

"Same as you, probably." He rumbled. "The area up there's been blocked off. The buses along this route were diverted. Has been for a few hours. A person could have gotten stranded. Got lost. Panicked." He trailed off as he scratched at his beard. "Still, we can't confirm anything yet. It might just have been a bear or something."

Alex wanted to argue that it was not a bear and that no one in their right mind would be hanging around in the forest, but here she was. Still, she was on the road, not in the middle of a forest. She opened her mouth to say so, but the words that left her mouth weren't the ones she had expected.

"How long ago did this happen?"

"About five or six hours ago, maybe." He turned to Detective Li. "I'll call it in." He repeated as he marched to the driver's side. He slid back in the driver's seat of the truck and began to talk over the radio attached to his dashboard.

Alex's jaws clamped down and she felt her back molars grind together.

She had seen something watching her. Whether or not it had anything to do with the other incident, she didn't know, but it was not a human she had seen.

As a child, she had spent her time reading books from *Littleton's library*, and while only a few of those books had been about animals she'd never seen an animal that had lights that resembled the ones she had seen. Not on land, at least. At best, the lights reminded her of the glowing lights of a flashlight fish. Or perhaps a cat sitting in the dark.

"Where were you heading?"

Alex looked up at the sound of Detective Li's voice. She had been staring blankly at Detective Lovett in his truck, lost in thought.

Detective Li repeated his question. "Where're ya heading?" The pleasant smile was still plastered on his face. "If it's near, we can probably just drop you off there."

Alex dragged her eyes away from Detective Lovett to look at Detective Li.

She didn't want to tell them she was moving, or where she was moving to. Over the years, she had learned not to tell everyone everything, no matter how kind they were. That had always proven to be the best choice for everyone involved.

Alex gave a small dismissive shrug as she searched around for a lie. Her eyes landed on the food wrappers. "Do you know the nearest place to grab something to eat? I was gonna stop off at a diner. I haven't eaten for the whole day. Been on the bus."

At the mention of food, her stomach rumbled and Detective Li's smile broadened. "We know a good place to get a burger. You like burgers, right?"

"Sure." She agreed though she had no idea what that was. It had to be some kind of food, right? She wouldn't say no to that.

He clapped his hands together and held his arm out towards the truck. "Ok, then, *Freddie's* it is. We'll drop you off there."

Alex hesitated. "Are you sure? I wouldn't want to waste your time."

"It's better that we don't leave you out here, right in the middle of nowhere to get mauled. Too much paperwork."

Alex didn't have a reason to disagree. Staying out in the cold and becoming stranded once again, surprisingly, didn't appeal to her.

Detective Li opened the back door to the truck and held it open for her. Alex ducked her head and slipped into the backseat, just as Detective Lovett finished his call. The heat circling the interior swarmed her as she entered, and the smell of cigar smoke filled her lungs, but she was too relieved to be out of the cold to care.

She fought the urge to cough as she took off her backpack and dropped it onto her lap. After taking a glance around to make sure that whatever was watching her hadn't doubled back to get her, she buckled her seatbelt and sat back as her eyes flicked back to the trees.

When she was satisfied that there wasn't anything lurking by the tree line, she turned to look at her driver, just as Detective Li slid into the passenger seat. Detective Lovett glanced back at Alex. "So, where can we drop you off?"

"We're taking her to *Freddie's Grill.*" Detective Li announced as he slammed the door behind him.

Detective Lovett nodded. "Alright, let's go."

Once Detective Li was buckled in, Detective Lovett started the truck and steered them away from the bus stop.

After a few minutes of driving in silence, Alex saw Detective Lovett's eyes settle on her in the rearview mirror. His eyes met hers in the reflection. "You meeting friends at Freddie's?" He asked her.

She shook her head. "No, it's just me."

There was a heavy pause before Detective Lovett spoke again. "We haven't seen you around before."

She folded her hands on top of her bag and gave Detective Lovett a tight-lipped smile. "I just moved. Getting used to everything." She shrugged at him in the rearview mirror as his eyes drilled into her. "So...what happened, exactly? You said an animal attack, but you're not sure. Who were they? How long ago did it happen? How did they-"

Detective Lovett held up a large hand and Alex clamped her mouth shut mid-sentence. "We don't know much yet. We're looking into it." He barked. Every word out of his mouth was clipped and left no room for questions or arguments.

Alex's eyes narrowed, as she stared ahead at the road that rushed towards them. "It must have been a pretty big incident to disturb the bus routes." She mused. Out of the corner of her eye, she saw Detective Lovett's hands twitch on the steering wheel.

The older detective took a weighted minute before Detective Li answered instead. "There were other instances of animal attacks in the past year. So that was the initial assumption tonight."

"But, you can't be sure?"

"There also has been an increase in other crimes too. Murders, and robberies to name a few. There have even been a few more missing cases. We- the police, that is- are handling it." Detective Lovett insisted. Steel was infused in every word.

"Isn't the incident that happened today a job for Animal Control?" Alex asked, her eyes flicking between the two of them.

Detective Lovett glanced at her in the rearview mirror again, before focusing his attention back on the road ahead. "Well, we've got them looking into things too. Once all the evidence has been collected and analysed, then we'll find out what happened. Until then..." He trailed off pointedly and they all fell into silence.

As they drove away from the wooded areas and down the road, towards busier streets, where the lights from the street lamps bounced off every surface in the truck. It drifted over the two men in the front seat, highlighting every crevice in Detectives Li and Lovett's faces. There were bags under both of their eyes, but they both remained focused and pensive.

The truck was uncomfortably quiet as they rushed through the streets. Detective Li turned back in his seat. "So, Alex, I forgot to ask, where're ya coming from?"

Alex's jaw flexed, and she ran a finger along the strap of her backpack. She hesitated for a second before she answered. "Oakland."

"Really?" Detective Li said in surprise. "Nice area. I got a cousin who lives over there."

Alex pressed her lips together to stifle a chuckle. She nodded in agreement. "Yeah. It's nice."

"You don't sound like it. Oakland." Detective Lovett rumbled.

Alex looked down at her fingers, as she picked at her nails. She knew that she didn't sound like an Oakland native. Every time she spoke, she stuck out like a sore thumb. Her accent was different, and she had been told that she enunciated her words too much. "Well, I'm not from Oakland originally."

"Where then?" He prodded.

"I've moved around a lot. Lived in many different places."

"Where are your parents from? Originally?" He continued, undeterred.

Alex's fingers found the strap on her backpack and started pulling at the frayed material. "I don't know." She admitted, with more bite in her words than she intended. "I've never met them." That was stretching the truth past its limits, but the truth was much more difficult to explain.

Besides, they didn't need to know everything.

Detective Lovett was silent for a moment. Alex didn't think he was going to say anymore, but he surprised her with his next words.

"This is not the safest neighbourhood to be in right now. You know that, right? Especially now. There are all sorts of people out there. You look like you barely clear five feet. I'm sure walking against a strong gale could cause you some problems. So, running around the neighbourhood, unarmed, especially at night isn't the best idea."

Alex had to stifle a scoff. She wasn't exactly unarmed, but she didn't think the cops needed to know that, either.

"I know, I just didn't have much choice. The bus took a little bit longer than I thought it would. It should have arrived hours ago."

"It's probably for the best," Detective Li interjected. He looked at his partner and lowered his voice. "If she had come down earlier, she might've ended up..." He trailed off, but neither Detective Lovett nor Alex forced him to continue.

Personally, Alex didn't want to think about what could have happened if they had shown up a few minutes later.

CHAPTER 3

Freddie's Grill shone like a beacon in the dark. The luminescent light that filled the interior of the restaurant, bled out and bathed the surrounding car park. Even as Detective Lovett's truck drove up to the parking lot, the light cut through the darkness to blind them.

Detective Lovett navigated the truck into the nearly packed parking lot, as he scanned the area for a space. He found one a few cars away from the main road and manoeuvred them into the tight space, as Detective Li and Alex rustled in their seats after forty-five-minute drive.

"Here we are." He announced as the engine died with a grumble.

Alex unbuckled her seatbelt, as she surveyed the parking lot and the illuminated building ahead of them. She unlocked the door and stepped out onto the tarmac, dragging her bag behind her. A chill rippled through her as she slammed the door behind her.

She had only managed to take a step towards the front of the truck before she noticed an older, red-haired woman striding towards them from across the parking lot.

The woman was somewhere in her mid-forties, or fifties, with dark auburn hair, pulled into a neat, silky ponytail at the base of her neck. Her willowy frame loomed over Alex, as she neared. Her hair whipped through the air with each step she took. The coal-black coat she wore was made from a thick, rich material and the matching hat and gloves she wore looked just as expensive. The rest of her clothes were also simple, but well-made. Her cheeks had gone beet red, but whether from the cold, from exertion, or from rage, Alex wasn't entirely sure. In her hands, was a stack of flyers that had been crushed in her tight grip.

Behind her was another, slightly younger woman with fairer hair who rushed to keep pace with the taller woman's long stride, but when the other woman marched with determination, she approached with apprehension. Her cheeks were also flushed, but this time it was clear that the cold was responsible. Her wide eyes skimmed over the scene in front of her and she slowed her pace until she came to a stop a few feet away from Detective Lovett's truck. She wasn't dressed for the cold. Her coat was a rich plum, and the material was expensive, but it was too short and light for the cold. The rest of her clothes were casual, but they wouldn't look out of place in a professional work setting. Over the crook of her arm was a black leather bag that looked ready to burst at the seams.

Though she had never seen either of these women before, Alex had initially assumed that the women had their attention on her. That is until the first woman reached near enough to the truck to be heard.

"Detective Lovett!" The woman snapped. Her voice was high and clear as it whipped through the air to lash out at him. She came to an abrupt stop in front of the driver's door. Her eyes flicked to Alex as she stepped past her before she glared down at Detective Lovett.

The weathered detective dragged a hand across his face with a laboured sigh. When he lowered his hand, Alex saw that the crease between his brows had deepened and cast a shadow over his eyes. His jaw was clenched and as he rested his hands back on the steering wheel, his fingers flexed ever so slightly and the tendons strained against the skin.

The woman folded her arms tightly over her chest as she towered over him, her dark blue eyes narrowed and piercing. The flyers in her hand were crushed underneath her arm, but she didn't seem to care. Her eyes flickered over every inch of him before she spoke again. "It doesn't surprise me that I found you here." She said, almost to herself. "Where else would our daring detectives be? Not following up any leads, that's for damn sure."

"Marcia..." Detective Lovett began patiently, as the other woman caught up to them.

The woman named Marcia ignored him, raising a gloved hand. "I've told you, time and again. I have spoken to all her friends. I've been keeping in touch with them, and they still don't know anything. She hasn't contacted them at all. That's not like her."

Detective Lovett deflated in exhaustion. "Marcia, I told you this morning. So far, no one else has seen her and it's not likely that anyone will if she's trying to lay low."

Marcia's jaw tightened. "And why would she try to 'lay low'?"

"Marcia..." The woman tried again, but Marcia remained undeterred.

39

"No! Why would she? Why wouldn't she call me!" Her voice rose to a shrill peak and the woman who had arrived with Marcia placed a hand on her arm, but Marcia yanked it away. The younger woman's eyes flashed as she pressed her lips together into a thin line, but when she spoke, her voice was soft and measured. "Maybe now's not the best time for this."

Marcia did not indicate that she had even heard the woman. "Someone must have picked her up, or talked to her." She continued. "If they saw her walking around, she must have taken the bus, or a train, or hitchhiked."

"That was almost a week ago. With every day it gets less and less likely that anyone will, especially if she decides to leave the area again. She'd be far away from Kenzo by now."

"I know all that, so why won't you do anything about it? The longer you wait..." Marcia sniffed. "I know my daughter, Detective. Better than anyone. She wouldn't have just picked up and left, I told you before. She would never do anything like this. It's been over a year and she hasn't even called."

Detective Li leaned over from the passenger's seat to address Marcia. "Her note says she wanted space. She's legally an adult and-"

"I don't care!" Marcia exploded. "I want you to find her! Now!" Though they had been alone in the parking lot, they had drawn the attention of a family of six that had just exited the diner. The father tugged the hands of the two youngest towards their car while the mother ushered the two older ones behind them, watching them warily.

Behind them, a white-haired woman in a faded blue coat walked from around the side of the building. She settled by the wall, covered by the shadow of the building, watching curiously at the confrontation in front of her.

Marcia noticed the attention and turned to their audience. "You'd better keep your kids close! Lord knows Kenzo's stellar police force won't be any use to you if they wander off too far!"

Her sharp voice lashed out to meet the oblivious family, and as one they all stared between Marcia and the truck, unsure how to respond.

The white-haired woman behind them, however, was unmoved. She was staring past Marcia and directly at Alex.

Her eyes roamed over Alex from head to toe, before both hers and Alex's attention was drawn back to the argument taking place in front of her as Marcia's voice raised in volume.

"Marcia, we aren't even the ones who deal with missing cases." Detective Li stated firmly, as Detective Lovett took a deep breath. "We spoke to the guys that do. Marie's an adult, and there's no reason to suspect that anything bad has happened to her. It's been over a week since someone last saw her. If she wanted to, she would have been in contact. I'm sorry, but there's nothing we can do."

"So, you're giving up?" Marcia whispered. "And I'm supposed to accept that?"

Detective Lovett kept his voice low and calm as he answered. "It's just like David said, we can't do much else. And Marie? She's a sensible young adult, with her head screwed on properly. I understand that it may be hard to see her go off but-"

"Don't you dare pretend that you care!" She hissed at him as her dark blue eyes flashed in a warning. "As long as your daughter is safe and sound, you don't care about anyone else's. If it was your daughter, Detective, you would do everything you could to get her back."

"Marcia... Watch it." Detective Lovett warned.

"That's not fair." The woman with Marcia added.

Henry's eyes snapped to her for a moment before he returned his attention to Marcia. "You need to stop there."

"Or else what? "Marcia's voice began to rise again. "My daughter is already gone! Yours is safe and sound! Mine's in some kind of trouble and you won't do a damned thing about it, just like you won't do a damned thing about anyone else!" She pointed a finger in the direction of the woman behind her. "According to Rachel, there are others that you're not even looking into. Other missing cases that I guess just aren't important enough."

"Marcia," Henry began again, but the woman in front of him continued.

"No, no, instead, you've been chasing a big dumb animal up and down Kenzo, wasting resources, when you should be catching thieves and murderers. Instead, you're chasing imaginary bears. Poetic, isn't it? Just another big, dumb, wasteful, animal chasing after another big, dumb wasteful animal. And you still haven't even seen it! So, I don't know how you expect to catch it. Yet, another mark of your incompetence! So, tell me, *Detective*, what's left for you to screw up? I might be safer in jail than out here, where you can't even protect the very people you're being paid to protect!" She screeched.

The whole parking lot had gone deathly silent and everyone was waiting to see what Henry would do next.

Alex swung her bag onto her back with a snort that cut through the silence and immediately caught everyone's attention.

Marcia whipped around to look at Alex. "Do you think this is funny?" She hissed.

"No. It's really not." Alex muttered as she fixed the straps of her backpack, ignoring the intense glare of the woman next to her.

"If your adult daughter left home, there isn't much he can do for her, legally, as Detective Li just stated. If she left a note, then that means she left on her own and isn't in any danger."

"Alex..."Detective Li warned, but Alex paid him no mind. The increasing rage burning in Marcia's eyes was too tempting to allow it to be doused so soon. That was a challenge Alex would happily accept.

"To me," she continued, "it just sounds like you and your daughter have a few issues to sort out, but those aren't police business. If she wanted to speak to you, she would. So, instead of questioning Detective Lovett's parenting, maybe you should question your own. After all, only one of you seems to know where their daughter is."

Blotches of red bloomed on Marcia's face as she glared down at Alex with a burning fury. Though she stood still, her body was vibrating with unused energy. Her hands twitched and she opened her mouth to retaliate, but the woman next to her stepped in between the two of them.

"Marcia, seriously." The woman whispered.

"Let's just all calm down." Detective Lovett insisted, looking between Alex and Marcia.

"Let's just put this behind us." Detective Li glared at Marcia, his smile nowhere to be seen.

Marcia broke off her heated glare from Alex and scoffed at the two detectives. Her eyes were wild with disbelief and her unleashed anger. "You want me to just forget that my daughter's missing? Just forget that fact?"

"She's not missing," Alex mumbled under her breath. "She ran."

Marcia's head snapped towards her and she took a step towards her, but again, the other woman stepped in between the two of them. "Marcia!"

"Go on," Alex goaded her, tilting her cheek up towards her, "but be careful. Your next move might end up wasting police resources."

Marcia inhaled shakily. Without a word, she glared once more at Detective Lovett, before she stormed away from them. She crossed the parking lot and climbed into a large silver car parked directly opposite them, before her car peeled away from *Freddie's* with the same brisk, impatience that had brought her to them.

The woman she had called Rachel, whom she had abandoned in the middle of a parking lot, didn't seem too bothered by the turn of events. If anything, she looked relieved to be away from Marcia. Her brow had creased, but her mouth had settled into a satisfied smirk.

Rachel turned towards Alex and the detectives in the truck, and suddenly, the corners of her mouth turned down, morphing her face into an apologetic grimace. "I'm so sorry. She didn't mean all of that. She's just concerned. It was Marie's birthday back in December. She hasn't heard from her daughter in over a year and she feels like no one is listening to her."

"Is that what you do? Listen to her?" Detective Lovett snapped. "And after you finish your article, then what? Is she still gonna have your sympathetic ear and a shoulder she can cry on?"

Rachel crossed her arms over her chest, with a frown. "Detective Lovett, you know that I-"

Detective Lovett barked a humourless laugh. "Oh, you bet I know. I know how you work too well." He growled, as his fingers twisted the key in the ignition.

The truck roared to life as Detective Lovett began to reverse his truck out of the parking lot. He glanced once at Alex. "Travel safe." He called out to her. Next to him, Detective Li raised a hand as a goodbye. Alex returned it as she and Rachel watched them drive away.

There was silence in the parking lot. The family had slipped away in their car and the white-haired woman was nowhere to be seen.

"That wasn't particularly pleasant," Rachel muttered.

Alex restrained the desire to roll her eyes. Considering the company that Rachel seemed to be keeping, Alex didn't want to spend any more time talking with her. Instead, she turned back to the diner. Since she was there, she decided she should eat.

She only managed to take one step in its direction, before Rachel stepped in front of her. The move didn't block Alex's way entirely, but Rachel had made it clear enough that she had something she wanted to say.

She gave Alex a small, but bright smile. The performative sympathy of the gesture was enough that Alex thought about stepping around Rachel altogether, but her curiosity kept her from leaving.

"You kinda got dragged into that just now." Rachel began slowly. "I'm sorry for that. Tempers got a little heated. I guess that's what happens when it comes to family."

Alex stayed quiet as she waited for Rachel to make her point.

"Marcia's-"

"Looking for her daughter." Alex finished impatiently. "Yeah, I caught that part."

Rachel adjusted her bag on the crook of her arm and nodded. "Yeah, and she came to me to make sure that the police are doing everything they can. That they're staying on the case and not brushing it aside."

"But she's not missing."

Rachel sighed. "The situation is a little...strange. I think some things are being overlooked."

"Like what?"

Rachel grimaced. "I don't think I can tell you that. It's still an ongoing investigation."

"Didn't sound like it. But you're, what? Trying to make sure they're doing their job?"

"Yes."

"And how are you doing that? By writing an article?"

Rachel scoffed dismissively, her smile flickering. "I'm a reporter for *Mercury News*. My name's Rachel Ellis. You might have read an article or two of mine. Writing articles to shed a spotlight on ways to help the community is part of my job."

Alex pursed her lips and shrugged. "Never heard of it. Or you."

Rachel's sympathetic smile faltered completely. "Look, I just want to help Marcia find her daughter, Marie. Making sure that the police are doing their job does that."

"Ending up in a cell next to her isn't what I'd call helpful," Alex muttered.

Rachel narrowed her eyes in disapproval. "Neither was provoking her in front of the police."

Alex squared her shoulders and matched Rachel's gaze until Rachel looked away with a shake of her head.

"Anyway, this is the first time I've seen her so angry. I didn't know it would escalate so quickly or so far."

While irritating and somewhat unreasonable, Marcia's outburst was, still, in some way understandable, Rachel's silent encouragement seemed more self-serving. All she had done was fuel the panic and paranoia of an already paranoid mother.

Reluctantly, Alex turned to Rachel. "Alright. What do you want with me?"

The abrupt change in the topic had Rachel startled but quickly schooled her expression to give some semblance of being detached from the subject. "What makes you say that?"

Alex shifted on her feet impatiently. "You're still talking to me."

"Just making conversation."

Alex nodded, unconvinced. "Alright, then. Bye."

She only managed to take a step away before Rachel stepped in front of her again.

"Ok, I wanted to talk." Her eyes skimmed over Alex thoughtfully. "You're about Marie's age, you know? Eighteen, nineteen years old."

Alex wasn't exactly sure how old she was any more. She'd lost track over the years, but her best guess was that she was in her mid-twenties, at the very least.

Rachel peered into Alex's eyes, trying to see if her words were reaching her, before roaming over the rest of her body, raking over her worn clothes and the large bag on her back. "Marcia says that Marie's not with any family members, and the only friends she has are here in Kenzo. She didn't have a lot of personal funds. So, I guess you can see why she's worried. Her only daughter's out in the world. Living rough. Alone. And for some reason, she's not contacting Marcia."

Alex suppressed the desire to scoff again, at the blatant attempt to appeal to her and reframe the situation she had just witnessed. Instead, she waited stonily for Rachel to continue.

Rachel sighed again and reached into her bag. From between an assortment of files, she pulled out a notebook packed with extra pages of torn-out articles and old leaflets. She fished through her book until she found a photo. Her mouth twisted into a grimace before she handed it over. She pointed at the girl on the left. "This is Marie Rosen. The other girl is her friend, Nina."

With a tired sigh, Alex plucked the photo from Rachel's fingers.

Though her hair was a few shades darker and her eyes were light brown, instead of navy blue, the girl Rachel had indicated in the photo was almost identical to Marcia. They both had long, narrow faces and sharp noses with pointed chins, but their eyes were hooded and round. She grinned lazily at the camera as she and her friend, Nina held up peace signs. Nina had brown hair with a reddish tint and her jaw was wider and more rounded. She smirked at the camera, with her arm wrapped around Marie's neck, pulling her close.

Alex handed the picture back with a shake of her head. "I've never seen either of them before. Sorry." She fiddled with the strap on her shoulder and took a step around Rachel.

Again, Rachel stepped in her path. "Well, have you seen other teens on the road? Spoken to them, maybe?"

"No."

Rachel sighed. She fished into her bag again and this time, she pulled out a small card. "Look, I get it. You don't want to get in the middle of anything. I understand. I've been looking into cases of missing people from all around

Kenzo. Cases that the police aren't doing anything about. A lot of them are teens, young adults with nowhere to turn. Around your age. I know you think no one else will understand, or listen to you, but I'm here if you need someone to talk to." She held the card out to Alex.

Alex resisted the urge to roll her eyes and with a small huff, she plucked the card from Rachel's fingers. The cream, rectangular card had 'Rachel Ellis' and various ways to contact her stamped in black ink. Alex pocketed the card.

"Sure." She mumbled as she walked around Rachel towards the diner, the card and the offer to help already discarded in her mind.

CHAPTER 4

In the end, Alex only stayed at *Freddie's* long enough to eat the 'house meal', as her waitress, Bea, had called it. A burger and fries with a large glass of a dark sweet drink that kept fizzing. The burger had been a slab of meat between two slices of bread. After the first bite, she could see why there were so many wrappers for *Freddie's* in the back of Detective Lovett's truck. Her stomach had growled impatiently even after she ate the last bite and for a moment, she contemplated buying another. A glance at her watch was the only thing that convinced her to step out of the diner and head back outside.

According to Bea, there was a nearby bus stop that would take her all the way to Troye. Thankfully, the roads were busier than the one she had been stuck at for ages.

Now that she was fed and somewhere populated she felt more confident and adventurous, but she kept her head down, and walked down the street the waitress had mentioned.

As the warmth from the *Grill* bled away and was replaced with a cold chill once again, she burrowed her hands deeper in her pockets and picked up her pace. She kept her mind from wandering back to the events of the past hour by focusing on reaching Troye.

After a few minutes of walking, Alex felt the familiar sensation of the hair on the back of her neck raising up. She looked around without breaking her speed, but she couldn't see anyone behind her. A seed of dread buried itself in the pit of her stomach and blossomed out, but she kept her pace until she reached the bus stop.

The metal of the shelter shone in the lamplight that circled it. The pavement below was clean and free from refuse, both natural and man-made.

She barely had a chance to come to a complete stop before a bus crested the hill to meet her. It was only as she boarded that she caught a glimpse of a figure, almost hidden in the shadows of the trees, watching her. As the bus pulled away from the curb, she peered into the dark and saw the white-haired woman from *Freddie's* pottering along the pavement. With an exhale, she collapsed into a seat at the back of the bus.

It took more than an hour for the bus to breach the boundaries of Troye. Once they neared the outskirts, the quality of the buildings severely decreased. Cracks crept through the stone of the buildings and the pavements that were lying down in front. Broken windows were boarded up and covered in dirt and grim. Abandoned buildings were increasing in number with every block they drove.

That would explain why the rent was so cheap.

Only ghosts lived there now.

And rats.

There was some kind of standard that buildings should be kept to, wasn't there? Was it a safe place for people to live? Looking at it from the outside, she doubted that. But, although the buildings looked ready to fall at the first sign of wind, she wasn't in a position to look for an alternative place to live. She hadn't even seen the place yet, so there was still hope. Besides, she couldn't afford anything else.

As soon as she saw the advertisement for the apartment, she knew she would have to take it, regardless of the state that it was in.

She rang the bell as the bus approached the next stop, and once the doors opened, she hopped off and took out her map again. Once she found the right streets, she sped off.

After a few more minutes of walking through the streets, *Cassandra's Palace* itself came into view out of the darkness, constructed in the middle of other smaller and much more dilapidated buildings. The name had been engraved into a plaque and nailed to the side of the building, and like everything else around it, the sign was ready to fall apart.

The building towered over her, casting her into shadow. Alex could see the large cracks in the stone walls, the ivy crawling around the building, and the broken windows that had been boarded up. A few of the windows had golden light spilling out from inside, showing that there was, at least, some life inside.

She walked along the cracked, dirtied sidewalk directly opposite the stone stairs that led up to the building's main entrance. She looked left and then right, as she crossed the wide road that had separated them from the building and jogged up the stone path to the main doors of the apartment complex.

She checked her watch again. It was now ten minutes to ten.

The wall to her left had a scratched metal panel that was clinging to the wall for dear life, holding on only by a screw or two. It had a keypad with the numbers 0 to 9, a few other labelled buttons, a small rectangular screen, speakers, and a small square to swipe something against. That last one was probably for an electronic key, for the residents to let themselves in.

But Alex hadn't been given any keys.

As her mind whirled through her limited options, her eyes caught sight of one of the buttons. It had been marked as 'office'. Though it was late, and Alex didn't expect anyone to answer, with no other options, Alex pushed the button.

The cold metal almost burnt the tip of her finger as they connected. The button resisted her, but she continued to push until she could feel the joints in her finger ache under the pressure and the sound of a buzzer rang through the air.

After a few seconds, she heard a man's voice. It was sluggish but melodic as it answered at the other end. "What do you want?" It snapped.

Relief surged through her and her words tripped over each other as they left her mouth. "Er, sorry, I...um, my name is Alexandria Raffaello. I-I'm looking for Vincent Sullivan. I'm renting apartment 14," she called into the receiver, "and I-"

Before she could say any more, there was a sharp scoff at the other end and a buzz rang out as the main doors unlocked to let her in.

She pulled the brass handles of the heavy wooden door and slipped inside into the inky darkness beyond.

CHAPTER 5

Alex crossed the threshold of the dilapidated apartment complex and stopped just inside the entrance, waiting as her eyes adjusted to the surrounding darkness.

As they did, she saw that beyond the interior expanded to a large main entrance. On the right side of the entrance was a bulletin board positioned above a table, with a bench beside it and next to that was a wall filled with mail slots. The other side of the entrance led to an even darker and smaller corridor.

Lining the walls of the corridor were four doors. Two on the right wall and two on the left, with the brass apartment numbers screwed onto the doors., the numbers marking them from 1 to 4.

At the end of the corridor, along the left side, was a metal staircase next to another door. A door had been left ajar, with a soft orange glow bleeding out from under it. As she watched, a shadow moved from behind.

Alex shuffled towards the door to keep herself from tripping in the diminished light. Even so, she could still see the discoloured carpets underneath her feet and the paint peeling off the walls on either side of her. It seems like no one had bothered to try to clean an inch of the place or maintain it for at least a decade.

Well, apart from the office.

The light seeping out of the office illuminated the surrounding area. Someone had bothered to clean the door and the walls on either side of it. They had scrubbed the carpet and walls to perfection within a foot of it. Beyond that, the dirt and dust accumulated with no issue.

Alex came to a stop just outside of the office as she heard someone rustling around inside.

The owner had installed a metal plaque on the front of the door. *Vincent Sullivan's Office.*

Alex tapped her knuckles against the door and, after another grunt, a man opened it wider.

Vincent Sullivan, the landlord, was a lot taller than Alex had expected.

He had a full head of dark hair, neatly trimmed, piercing grey eyes and a sharp face. He was considerably taller than Alex, but still very wiry. He wore a crisp, navy blue shirt that was folded back by the elbows, displaying the muscles that corded around his arms as he crossed them over his chest. He sucked at his teeth in irritation.

Despite the state of the property he owned and presumably maintained, he at least looked well taken care of.

His eyes swept over Alex from head to toe. "The new tenant?"

Alex crossed her arms over her chest. "Yeah. Apartment 14."

His jaw worked, and he frowned as his eyes continued their appraisal. He nodded once and stepped back into his office for a moment before he returned with a set of keys. He handed them to Alex by the ring connecting them. "As I stated before, your apartment is already furnished. Follow me."

He closed his office door behind him and led her back down the corridor and to the left, where a staircase was tucked away, out of sight. She hadn't seen it when she entered the building and only saw it now that she stood directly in front of his office.

They climbed the flight of stairs and turned off onto the third floor. Alex followed him silently to the end of the hallway, past a few other doors. He stopped in front of a door on the left at the very end of the corridor, in front of a large frosted window that allowed soft light in.

He turned and presented the door of apartment 14 to her with a flick of his wrist. "If you need anything, feel free to call." He said monotonously. Before she said anything else or could think of a question to ask him, he turned and sauntered back down the hallway, leaving only his echoing footsteps behind.

Alex turned back to her door. It had been painted a dark brown with a brass number "14" underneath a peephole. Looking around, she could see that the surrounding doors were the same.

Alex placed the key in the lock and turned it, but it stuck where it was. She turned it harder and pushed until finally the door unstuck and creaked open.

The darkness of the room blinded her. Alex blinked rapidly as her eyes struggled to adjust, taking in the dark mass of shapes in front of her.

She stepped inside her new home and closed the door behind her. The little light that had drifted in from the hallway to illuminate the room was shut out and she was engulfed in darkness. She stretched out a hand towards the wall and felt along it until she found the light switch and flicked it on.

The dull artificial light filled the room to reveal a surprisingly large living room connected to a kitchen with a stove, fridge and microwave. In front of her, to the left and the side of it along the left wall, were two doors. The walls were a muddy white, and the curtains were a cheap blue material and it was frayed at the bottom.

The room had all the basic furniture. Two chairs, a table, a couch and a stove. They came with the flat and didn't seem like they cost too much. It was enough. She could go shopping for the rest of the essentials that she needed.

Alex walked to the door directly opposite her. She opened it to find a bathroom on the other side, with an old toilet, a sink and a bath along the wall with a shower curtain hiding it from view.

She walked to the other door and opened it to find a bedroom. In the middle of the room, there was a bare single bed, a dirty white dresser next to it, and a small wooden wardrobe in the corner.

Alex's eyes scanned the room twice before she placed her bag at the foot of the bed.

She walked back into the living room area and sighed as she took off her coat. She draped it over the back of the couch and collapsed on top of the cushions.

This was the first chance she had in hours to rest. Despite everything that she had been through since morning, she felt safe. The shadows looming from the woods were a distant memory and growing further away.

The eyes...

Despite the dull pit in her stomach that warned her otherwise, she wanted to forget what she had seen. It wasn't her business. It wasn't her problem. There was nothing she could do. At least, that's what she would use to comfort herself.

Now that she was inside, as she thought back to what she had seen at the bus stop, she couldn't be sure what she saw.

It was too late at night, and she wanted to move on to another, calmer day.

She kicked off her shoes and brought her knees to her chest as she curled up on the couch, her eyes closing almost instantly as she settled into the cushions beneath her.

Alex woke up a few hours later in her darkened apartment. Her mouth stretched into a yawn as she looked around, scratching her head. She swung her feet off the couch as she sat up and checked her watch.

It was a quarter to four in the morning.

She stood up, stretched, and shuffled her way to the bedroom on unsteady feet.

It was much colder in there than in the living room, now that she was only wearing a thin t-shirt and jeans.

She picked up her backpack and began rummaging through it. Inside, she found the small notepad and pen she kept tucked in between the few books she owned and opened it to a fresh page. She pulled the cap of the pen off with her teeth, chewing on it absently. There were things that she needed to buy, but she wasn't sure where to start.

Alex looked around her, at the sparse room she stood in for a moment, searching for inspiration.

The open door of her bedroom drew her attention. She went in and made a list of everything that came to mind. When she had finished, she made her way to the bathroom.

After taking note of the items that she already had in the apartment in her head, she started writing down the ones she needed to buy on the list.

Bedsheets, for the bed, since she didn't have any of her own.

Curtains for the windows, since she preferred to sleep in complete darkness.

Cleaning products to clean the entire apartment since if the exterior of the building and the hallways were any indications, she'd need it.

She walked out of the room and into the bathroom. Again, the space was surprisingly large, just neglected.

Alex chewed on the cap even harder, her brow furrowing. She didn't know why the rent was so cheap if the apartment was so big.

Were the other apartments like that, too?

If Vincent bothered to maintain the complex, each apartment would be worth a lot more than what Alex had paid for it. The cost to clean and keep the building updated would be far less than what Vincent stood to gain.

Not that she was complaining.

But there had to be something that Alex wasn't aware of yet. There had to be a catch. She just hoped it was one she could afford to deal with. But in the meantime, she would be grateful for what she had.

She added more items to her list as she walked around the apartment. Shower curtains, bathroom cleaning supplies, a kettle, cups, plates and cutlery. There was already a fridge, a microwave and a stove in the kitchen area. A table and couch in the living area. A bed in the bedroom.

Alex knew she probably needed a lot more, but she was sure that she had covered the essentials. The rest she'd get in time.

There was a decent amount of money she had saved up. She'd calculated that she'd had enough to cover rent and food for at least a few months.

Absently, she took the pen cap out of her mouth, wiped it off on her t-shirt and stuck it back on the pen.

While Alex did enjoy her luxuries, she had spent most of her life making do with less, so she was quite confident that she'd be fine. Things were better than she'd expected.

She went back to her room and dropped the notepad and pen back in her bag, and instead took out her bag of toiletries, a towel, and clean clothes.

Out of the corner of her eye, she saw her notepad again and paused for a second before she grabbed it again and added a few more items that came to mind. She tapped the end of the pen on her lip as she hummed to herself.

Her eyes drifted to the pile of clothes in front of her. She would have to figure out where the nearest laundromat and supermarket were. She scribbled down a note to do so before she dropped the notepad and pen back into her bag and headed for the bathroom.

The shower was only five minutes long since the water fluctuated between scolding and freezing. Most of the water had ended up on the floor, thanks to the way they had installed the shower head and the shower curtain made of tissue paper.

If Alex had to guess, she would bet that Vincent had bought and installed it himself.

She was sure that a few days of living in the apartment would reveal the issues that hadn't been mentioned in the advert.

Still, it could be worse.

It had taken another five minutes to dry off, clean up the water from her shower, and get ready. As she passed a brush through her wet hair, her stomach rumbled again. She tied her hair up and went back to her bag.

Sticking her hand inside, she found the sandwich she had packed before leaving the morning before. She unwrapped it, took a bite and, once again, she picked up her notebook, adding 'food shopping' to her list.

As she ate, Alex walked back through the living room and to the kitchen area. She opened the cupboards to see how much space she had before moving to the fridge and checking there. They were both somewhat clean, but she would need to stand on a chair to reach the cupboards to see on top.

The cupboards would probably never be full entirely, but it was good to know that she had the space if she needed it.

When Alex finished her sandwich, she turned to the table with two matching wooden chairs.

She pulled them out with a loud scrape against the floorboards and got on her knees to inspect underneath. Again, they were relatively clean, but considering the state of the built-in furniture that had come with the apartment, Alex now realised that this was probably more to do with the last tenant than it was to do with Vincent.

She got up and pushed the seat of one chair, putting most of her weight onto it. It resisted her. She picked up the chair, placed it in front of the kitchen cabinets, and stepped on the seat. Her head barely reached above the cabinets on the walls, but she could see the dust that had accumulated there.

She stepped back down on the floor and pushed the chair back to the table, looking around at her home.

She could work with this.

This could be her home.

All she would need to do is lay low and mind her own business.

Once she had come to the end of the inspection of her new apartment, Alex put the chair back where she had found it, and walked back to the couch.

As she did so, she glanced out of the window opposite her. She had done so out of reflex, as sudden movement across the pavement below caught her attention. The flimsy curtains across the windows barely covered them and stood in front of her couch. She could see the road that ran alongside *Cassandra's*. Though, now that she was paying attention, she couldn't see anything moving outside. She rubbed her eyes and looked again, but her eyes swam in the darkness and she couldn't be sure if she had seen anything at all.

Despite trying to keep it far from her mind, the fear that she had felt at the bus stop had been real, and it had followed her home.

KENZO

She peeked out through the curtain and saw a shadow lurking on the pavement below and disappeared into the darkness. She stepped back from the window and took a deep breath as she rubbed at her tired eyes.

She closed her eyes. It was just a figment of her imagination. She was safe in her new home. No one knew her. She was safe.

It had been such a long day and there was no reason to make it longer.

She collapsed back on the sofa and, as soon as her head hit the cushion, fell straight back to sleep.

CHAPTER 6

Alex woke up a few hours later, sprawled out on the couch, the fingertips of her left hand brushing the ground, as the pale rays of the sun licked at her skin. As she stirred, she blinked against the light. A yawn stretched her jaw wide open and her back arched like a cat. She sat up, swinging her legs off the seat, and she looked around the room for a moment, before she remembered where she was.

With another yawn, Alex shoved her feet back into the shoes she had discarded the night before, which were still sprawled on the floor next to her. She fixed her hair into a ponytail, grabbed her coat, bag, and her new keys, and exited her apartment, locking the door behind her.

It took three tries before the door slammed shut completely and even then, the lock still did its best to struggle against the key.

Once out of her apartment, she made her way along the dimly lit hallway and back down the staircase to the ground floor.

In the light of day, the main entrance of *Cassandra's Palace* was light and airy, if a bit dirty and run-down. The entrance was larger than it had looked at night and she could see it clearly as light filtered in through the windows.

Now, it looked almost friendly.

Once she was back out onto the street, in front of the crumbling complex, she looked up at the buildings surrounding her. With the sun out, she could make out the broken buildings that stood alongside *Cassandra's Palace* and the abandoned cars parked on the streets gathering dust.

A cold wind rushed past her, rustling the curls of her hair into her face. She brushed it back, and as she turned her head, out of the corner of her eye, she caught a glimpse of her reflection in the frosted glass of the windows of the *Palace*.

She could see a small young woman with hollow cheeks, dark circles under her dark eyes and a mess of curly black hair in a ponytail. The winter had turned her olive-toned skin a few shades lighter. She looked almost grey. The last time she checked her appearance in the mirror, she was more tanned. She was wearing a burgundy jacket that was way too big for her, jeans that had faded over years of use and an old green backpack that was more brown than green slung over her shoulders.

Alex looked down at her feet and her ratty shoes stared back up at her. The laces were frayed and muddy, and every time it rained, it was like stepping in a puddle.

She needed new clothes. There was enough wardrobe space for them.

Every item of clothing she owned was either on her or in her backpack and it had been that way for at least the past five years.

When was the last time she had even bought clothes?

She couldn't remember buying the ones she wore now.

Her stomach rumbled loudly, breaking her train of thought. She turned from her reflection, readjusted the bag on her back and walked back up the street that she had come down the night before.

On her way there she had seen a supermarket a few buildings away from a cluster of stores.

Right now, she needed food more than she needed clothes.

The walk to the supermarket felt much shorter during the day. There were very few people who were out at this time and there were even fewer inside the supermarket.

Alex grabbed a basket by the sliding doors and marched in. She moved from one aisle to the next, slipping past the other customers, snatching basic items, easy things to heat and eat, from the shelves and dropping them in her basket. She hated shopping and didn't want to spend more time than she had to in there. The quicker she left, the better her chances were of not being stuck in the middle of the morning rush.

She had just slipped between two other customers to pick up a carton of apple juice when she saw a familiar figure at the end of the aisle.

It took her a second too long to register that she was staring at Marcia Rosen. The woman was in the middle of shoving a flyer in the face of two other customers when she looked up and caught Alex watching her.

Alex looked away. She dropped her carton in her basket and turned to leave, but Marcia handed the couple the flyer and stalked over to Alex. With her longer legs, she easily caught up to Alex and blocked her way out of the aisle.

"You! You were with the detectives last night weren't you?" She snapped.

"Yeah," Alex mumbled, as her muscles tensed. Her spine stiffened to raise her head to Marcia's level, wary of what the woman might do next. Alex hadn't expected to see Marcia again, or so soon.

The older woman's eyes flickered for a moment before they focused on Alex. "Rachel said she spoke to you. She... she said that she spoke to you...about Marie."

Alex nodded, pulling back a step. "Yeah, she did."

Marcia nodded absently. "She said you might know something that might help."

Alex's eyes narrowed and her brows creased in confusion. "Look, I'm sorry, but I don't know-"

Almost unconsciously, Marcia took another step towards Alex, trying to bridge the gap between them, as if that would make Alex understand. Reflexively, Alex took a step back.

Marcia didn't seem to notice her discomfort and continued, almost as if the words were spilling out of her. "She says that you've been living rough, that you might have run away from home. Have you met any other girls living on the street?"

Alex took another step away, but Marcia took another to match her. They had backed out of the juice aisle and were now in the open. More people had flooded into the shop and were now looking at her and Marcia, but still, Marcia didn't seem to notice. Alex lowered her voice in an attempt to lose the attention they had unknowingly gained. "I'm sorry, I really don't know-"

"Marcia, honey, come on! You're scaring the girl." A low, smooth voice interrupted. Alex's attention was drawn away from Marcia, and over her shoulder to a tall chestnut-haired woman sauntering towards them from the other end of the aisle.

The brown pants suit she wore, alone, cost more than every item in that aisle. Add in the price of her coat and her high heels, and that would still be more than the supermarket would make in a month. With every step she took, her freshly-curled hair gleamed even in the artificial light.

"I'm so sorry," she insisted. She shot Alex a bashful, but dazzling smile, "my friend's not normally this lacking in manners. She's just..." she glanced at Marcia, who was staring off to the side, ignoring them both. "She's really worried about her daughter." She finished. "We wouldn't want to take up your time. We'll leave you alone." She held her hand out to Marcia.

When Marcia began to protest, the woman interrupted again. "Marcie, seriously, leave the poor girl alone." She beamed at Alex as Marcia glared at her. She extended her hand. "I'm Nicolette James. You?"

"Alex," Alex muttered.

"Well, Alex, I really hope you'll forgive us. As a parent, it's not easy to sit back and wait when it comes to your children. Especially when you think they're in danger." She looked down at Alex's basket. "How about, as an apology, I pay for that and we can just forget about all this?"

Alex's hand clenched around her basket. "No."

Nicolette's brow creased in surprise. She frowned down at Alex, while Marcia continued to glare.

Alex shifted uncomfortably. "I mean, it's fine. I'll pay for myself. No hard feelings."

For a second, Alex thought that would be the end of it, but Marcia opened her mouth again. "You spoke with the detectives. They must have told you something. You were defending them."

Alex shook her head as she tried to edge away. "They didn't, I'm sorry." Her eyes darted around, searching for an escape. She took a step to the right, but Marcia followed her and once again, stepped directly into Alex's path. Her right hand whipped out and latched on Alex's arm, trapping her in place. The floral scent of Marcia's perfume overwhelmed Alex's nose and she felt her blood boil as her tightly-wound nerves snapped. "Rachel said-"

Alex twisted her arm out of Marcia's grip and grabbed the other woman's wrist.

"Listen!" She hissed. Marcia tried to pull away but Alex held on. "I don't know anything about your daughter. I don't know what that woman, Rachel, told you, but she's wrong. She's just telling you what you want to hear so she can write her article. She doesn't care about you or your daughter. If she wanted to help you, she would tell you that you're wasting your time, because your daughter ran away from you. Now, you need to back off and stay away from me!"

She dropped Marcia's hand and took a step back from the woman. Marcia's eyes widened and she opened her mouth as tears filled her eyes, but she didn't say anything. Nicolette stood silently beside Marcia, her eyes scanning the area around them. Alex turned and saw that they were being watched by almost every customer standing in line for the till, and a few others milling around. Only the workers that passed by managed to act as if they heard nothing and carry on with their jobs.

It was clear that the other customers had seen the exchange between Marcia and Alex. Some of them held the same flyers that Marcia held clenched in her fist. A few turned back to their own business, pretending to have not seen anything.

Without a glance back, Alex took her basket and joined the line for the till. Behind her, she heard Nicolette whisper soothing words as she guided Marcia out of the supermarket.

As Alex waited in line, she heard whispered conversations all around her.

"...*you know I feel bad, sure. But you can't go around treating people like dirt and get surprised when they fight back...*"

"...*about time someone said it. We were just too polite to...*"

"...*if it was our daughter, she wouldn't care. People go missing all the time around here, but God forbid anything bad happens in Belamour. It rains and they want to sue...*"

"...was that Nicolette James? Like, THE Nicolette James? What the hell is she doing here in the middle of Annie's?"

"...still, that was kinda mean to say..."

"...she didn't give her a choice. She shouldn't have grabbed her..."

"...I feel so bad for that woman..."

"...I agree more should be done. She's not the only one. But, that girl had a point. Her daughter isn't missing, but other people are..."

Alex kept silent even as her items were scanned and bagged. She paid the money to the teller, picked up her bags and left the store, with the silent promise that she would never step foot in *Little Annie's Food Factory* again.

CHAPTER 7

An hour and a half later, Alex was scowling up at the stone steps of *Cassandra's Palace*, juggling her shopping between her two hands, and even her feet. Though there were only 10 steps at best from the pavement to the door, with her bags, the journey up the stairs felt like a hike up a steep mountain.

The events from the supermarket were still on her mind. She kept replaying everything, trying to recall the event properly. She wished it hadn't been so public.

It hadn't been her intention to humiliate Marcia, or herself, but both Marcia and Rachel had pushed her too far. She could understand Marcia wanting to find her daughter, but if she had chosen to leave, then Marcia's behaviour was too extreme.

Besides, if this was how she was on a regular basis, she didn't blame Marie for leaving.

And Rachel? Well, Alex wasn't entirely convinced that her motivations were altruistic either. Sure, she probably wanted to help 'make a change' as she put it, but her enabling a distraught woman on a wild goose chase would only ever end in heartache. It was cruel to make her think otherwise. Marcia might spend the next 20 years of her life looking for a daughter who would prefer to run from her. If she did find her, it wouldn't be a heartfelt reunion.

After she had left the supermarket, she wandered in and out of other neighbouring stores, becoming familiar with the area.

Though she hadn't been in the mood to mingle with other people, there were other essentials that she needed to buy. Luckily for her, she wouldn't have to travel far to find furniture, clothing or electronics, seeing as there was a large, grimy mall a few miles away from the supermarket, housing every type of store.

When Alex finally muscled her way into the lobby with all her bags in tow, she was surprised to find a group of people deep in the middle of a conversation. Two men, and two women, all over thirty had gathered in the lobby to talk. The door had announced her arrival like a foghorn and as one, their heads all snapped towards her, observing her with open interest as she approached.

"Need any help?" The taller man called out.

Alex shot him a polite smile but shook her head. "No, I'm good, but thank you."

He nodded and returned to their conversation as Alex regained her bearings. She juggled the bags in her hands to give her room to hold her keys. Once she had a better handle on them, she walked through the lobby to the back of the building.

On the bottom step of the staircase stood a tall, slender girl rummaging through her large leather bag. Whispered swears fell from her mouth every few seconds, that probably weren't for anyone to hear. Her long black hair spilt over her shoulders to tangle on her necklace, on the items inside her bag and on the zips along the outside of it. Whenever her hair snagged, her curses became more descriptive.

Despite the cold weather, she was wearing torn shorts, a faded, black baggy t-shirt with a print on the front, heavy boots and ripped black socks that reached the middle of her thighs. Bracelets rattled along her arms, punctuating her frantic movements.

"Come on!" She hissed as she dug deeper into her bag.

Alex hesitated a few steps away from the girl, but she hadn't noticed her presence. Alex cleared her throat. "Hello? Hi?" She called out.

The tall girl spun around, screamed and dropped her bag. It fell on the floor and sent everything inside flying across the floor.

"Oh, come on!" The girl hissed. She crouched down and started gathering her belongings from the ground.

Alex shuffled over to the girl. She put her bags to the side and crouched down next to her. There was a tube of mascara and a brush by her feet. She reached out and picked them up. "Sorry."

The girl huffed out a laugh that had very little humour in it. "Oh, no, don't worry. That was all me. I'm sorry. I'm just...just so stressed, you know? I said I'd help Duke today – even though it's my day off – but I need the money, you know? So I got up early to help him out, because it's not like I can really pass that up, right? Plus, he's a great boss. Anyway, I came home and now I can't find my keys. 'Cause, they're not in there. Because why would they be!"

Alex stared wide-eyed at the girl as she pressed her hands to her eyes. She shifted on the balls of her feet and her eyes darted to the stairwell behind the girl.

If only she could edge around her...

The girl sniffled and swiped at her nose before she raised her head suddenly and her eyes locked on to Alex. They were a vivid green, and shone like emeralds, even in the dull artificial light. "Hey, can I borrow your phone?" She stood up to her full height and took a step towards the stairwell, pointing toward the apartments above them. "I'll be quick. I'll pay you back, or whatever, I promise." She clasped her hands together in front of her.

Alex stood up from her crouch and collected her bags. "I-I don't have a phone line set up, sorry," Alex admitted. One of the things she hadn't bought was a phone. Since she had no one to call, phone service was low on her list of priorities.

The girl sighed. "Ok." She rubbed her bottom lip before she dug her front teeth into the flesh absently. "Payphone." She mumbled. "There's one across the road." She tutted and threw her hands in the air in defeat. Her bracelets rattled angrily with the movement. "Forget it. He should be home soon."

"Who?"

"Spencer. He lives in the building too." Her eyes focused back on Alex and she frowned. "Wait, do you live here?" She gestured vaguely at the building around them. "I've never seen you here before."

"I'm new. Moved in last night." Alex juggled her bags in her hand. The handles were pulling at her skin. Every step she took challenged the bag's tenuous connection with its handles.

She hoped that this would be the end of the conversation and the girl would lose interest and move on to other things. Maybe if Alex stood still long enough without saying anything, she'd leave on her own. With any luck, she would forget all about Alex the moment she lost sight of her.

The girl looked down at her and smiled toothily. She held out her hand and again, the bracelets on her wrists jingled as she moved. "I'm Marigold. Goldie's fine, though."

Alex moved her keys and her bags to her left hand, took Goldie's and shook. "Alex."

Goldie grinned. "Good shake! Dad says that's a good sign. Of what? I'm not sure. But, anyway, it's nice to meet you."

"You too."

Goldie froze for a second, as her eyes narrowed. Slowly, Goldie retracted her hand and scurried away from the stairs, down to the end of the hall, to Vincent Sullivan's office. "Oh!" She exclaimed. "Give me a minute." She called back over her shoulder.

Reluctantly, Alex stood in the entrance hall, her arms crying in pain under the weight of her bags, as Goldie rapped her knuckles against the door of their landlord's office.

She waited, for a moment with her ear pressed against the door, before she knocked again.

"Sully? Please? It's Marigold. I got locked out again. I need the spare key!" She waited again, but there was no answer.

Alex cast the staircase next to her a longing stare, but she stayed where she was.

Goldie deflated against the door and banged again. "Sully!"

Alex took a step forward and raised her voice so that Goldie could hear her. "I don't think he's in." She added unhelpfully.

Goldie banged her head against the door. "I know." She wailed.

"I thought you said that your friend, Spencer, was coming back soon."

"Yeah, but I wouldn't have to wait if my dick of a landlord would give me another spare key, but he won't because he's a dick!"

"But..he's not in."

Goldie scoffed and put her hands on her hips. "Well, it's kinda 50-50 with that guy. You think he's not there, and maybe he's not, but sometimes I think he's just pretending he can't hear us so he doesn't have to do his job. He's probably sitting at his desk, staring at the door." Her eyes widened and she turned to Alex. "Do you know anything about picking a lock?"

"No!" Alex hissed as her fingers itched. "I'm not helping you to break into our landlord's office! It's only my second day here!"

Goldie waved the idea away. "No! I meant for my apartment. If you could break in, I'd never need to worry about getting locked out again."

Alex closed her eyes as her head began to pulse. "You said your friend...Spencer, right...he would be back soon and I'm guessing he has a spare key?"

Goldie nodded reluctantly and sighed. "Yeah, well, thanks, anyway. I guess I'll...just wait for him, then." She checked the watch on her wrist and dragged her hands through her hair and down her face. Her eyes drifted to the left and lost their focus before they locked onto Alex once again. "Give me another minute." She whispered before she marched back down the hallway, past Alex and into the foyer.

"Hey, guys." She announced to the group still standing there. The group of people were still talking amongst themselves but they looked up as Goldie swept past them, their eyes drifting back towards Alex as she hovered by the entrance. "Whatcha talkin' 'bout?" She sang as she walked to a wall full of mailing slots and opened one of them.

A dark-haired woman pursed her lips. "The same thing we were talking about before."

"Ah, I see," Goldie mumbled as she took out a pile of letters from the slot. Her eyes skimmed over the windows of the letters, flicking through them before she looked over her shoulder at the group and smirked. "You think if we bitch about him enough he'll show up?" She teased.

The tall man that had offered to help Alex chuckled. "If that was the case he would've been here half an hour ago."

The dark-haired woman shook her head and crossed her arms tight over her chest. "I don't even know what I'm going to do about my boiler. We haven't even seen Mr Sullivan in weeks. I keep trying to call him. Leaving messages, notes, and emails for him, but he only says that he'll deal with it 'soon'. That was at least two weeks ago and my apartment is freezing."

Next to her, a woman with light brown hair hummed in disapproval. "When I took the kids to school this morning his car was in the parking lot. In the same spot in the back, but when I checked again, it was gone."

The shorter man looked down at his watch. "Damn. Wendy and I were supposed to be leaving for a vacation with the kids. Gotta go pack up our stuff and get the kids ready. The sink needed fixing before we came back. You don't suppose it will be done by then, do you?"

Goldie and the group gave a humourless chuckle. The dark-haired woman turned towards the main door. "Well, have fun. I have to get to work."

The group began to disperse in different directions. The tall man nodded and patted the shorter man on his shoulder. "Same. Talk to you later."

They all called out their goodbyes and left. The two men and the dark-haired woman walked out through the main doors, while the brown-haired woman turned and walked back up the stairs.

Goldie puffed out a breath. She glanced down at the stack of mail in her hand and sighed. Alex had only time to turn to the stairwell as the brown-haired woman walked past before Goldie spoke again. "What apartment do you live in?"

Alex gritted her teeth. "14." She called over her shoulder, as she began walking up the stairs only to hear Goldie's boots clattering right behind her.

"Seriously? Number 14?"

Alex slowed her pace and turned back to look at Goldie. Though Goldie was a step below hers, she was still taller than her. "Is that a problem?"

Goldie's mouth twitched but she shook her head as they climbed higher. "Sorry. I'm just surprised anyone took that apartment, after what happened to the last tenant."

Alex frowned in confusion. "I'm sorry. What happened to the last tenant?"

Goldie sighed heavily, but her voice stayed light and airy. "Well, she was killed by that animal running up and down Kenzo."

Alex paused. "Was she killed in the apartment?"

Goldie scoffed. "Oh, god, no! She was out hiking or something when she got attacked. How the hell would an animal get in here anyway?"

Alex shrugged. "Huh." Alex didn't want to sound insensitive but if the woman didn't even die in the apartment, she didn't see what the problem was. Sure, it was grizzly but, there were probably many apartments and houses that were bought where the previous occupant had died before, whether through natural causes or not.

As if Goldie had read her mind, she continued. "Sure, it might not be a big deal, but I guess I just didn't expect that the apartment would be back on the market so soon after she died. Funny how quickly Sully moves when money's involved."

With a bitter chuckle, Goldie turned and continued walking up the stairs.

There was silence between the two as they walked, but Alex could sense that Goldie still had a few more questions on her mind.

"When did you say you got here?" She asked after a while.

"Last night."

"Okay. Well, you live opposite Spencer. You know, that friend I told you about?" She added. "He lives just below me. He's the one with my spare key. I'm pretty sure that today's his day off work so he should be back soon. Have you two met?"

"No. I haven't had a chance to meet anyone yet." And she didn't want to, especially after what had just happened earlier.

Once they had arrived on the third floor, Alex shuffled to her front door. She pulled out her key and slotted it into the lock. With a shove, the door swung open and she stepped into her apartment.

"You're gonna have to get used to things like that," Goldie said, pointing at the door as she sauntered across the threshold. "Trust me, no matter how many times you try to track Sully down, nothing in this place ever gets fixed." She cast her gaze around the room before she collapsed onto the couch, with a clatter of bangles.

Alex glared at the side of Goldie's head and slammed the door behind her. "I guessed as much." She dropped her bags behind the couch and slipped her backpack off her back.

Outside the door, the chatter of two men conversing with each other drifted through the closed door, as they both made their way up the stairs to Alex's floor.

At the sound, Goldie stood up and rushed to the door, past Alex. She yanked it open again and hurried out into the hall. Curiously, Alex stuck her head out after her.

Two men were in the middle of a conversation when they arrived on their floor. One was a tall blond man with glasses, wearing a white shirt and jeans and the other, was a taller, dark-skinned man in overalls.

"Thank God!" Goldie exclaimed as soon as she saw them.

Both men looked up in their direction. Their eyes landed on Goldie and then moved to Alex. The taller man propped his hand on the railing. "Mornin' Goldie." He rumbled cheerily. "And what are you after'?"

Goldie raised a hand in greeting. "Hey, Greg. I was just looking for Spencer. My...wonderful, dear, dear friend."

Spencer glared at her through his glasses. "What is it?"

Goldie gave him a sheepish smile. "I got locked out."

"Oh, no," Spencer muttered dryly. "Because that's never happened before. It's unheard of. An anomaly."

"Oh, shut it, asshole. I'm not in the mood. You're lucky that Alex was nice enough to keep me company while I waited for your slow ass to get me back into my apartment." She held out a hand to present Alex. "Alex, this is Greg," she gestured to the taller, darker man in overalls, "and this is Spencer." She gestured to the man with blond hair and glasses.

Alex shrank away from the curious looks of Greg and Spencer. "Hi." She offered.

"Hello." The two men answered back.

Spencer's eyes flicked up towards Goldie. "I'll get your spare keys. Give me a second." He strode down the hall to his apartment opposite Alex's. He slotted the keys into the lock with a practised flick of his wrist and shouldered the door open. The sound of heavy footsteps echoed in the air, followed by the sound of scraping furniture.

Goldie blew strands of hair out of her face and smiled up at Greg. "So, Greg. Alex just moved in last night, just opposite Spence in apartment 14."

The corners of Greg's mouth pulled down and his brow creased at the news. "Nice to meet you. I was just telling Spencer that tomorrow night the residents are having a meeting in Angela's bookstore. You know, to just talk about issues we have with the building, things like that. You'll have a chance to meet everyone there."

Goldie raised her eyebrows in surprise. "Really? I thought Angela was having trouble pinning down Sully. How did she find him?"

Greg shoved his hands in his pockets as he scowled. "She couldn't. But she left a note on his door, a note *under* his door, a message on his office phone, and a message on his *cell phone*. There's no way he would have missed it. Whether or not he shows up is something else entirely."

Goldie shook her head. "This is the first time I'm hearing about it."

Greg scratched his ear uncomfortably. "Well, I guess she spent so much time trying to track him down, she forgot to tell everyone else. That's why I'm here. She told me to make sure that everyone shows up tonight."

"Well, we'll be there," Goldie said firmly. Alex pressed her lips firmly together. She hoped that Goldie was only talking about Goldie and Spencer, but the pit in her stomach told her she was being hopelessly optimistic.

Spencer stepped out of his apartment, the keys jingling merrily in his hands. "I don't see the point of the meeting. Sully's not gonna be there. Even if we wrote a petition, he would still ignore us." When he was close enough, he tossed the keys to Goldie. She caught them deftly in one hand and turned them over.

"Thanks. Doesn't Sully have to beef up security or something? I mean, someone died." She winced and glanced back at Alex for a second before continuing. "There should be CCTV, shouldn't there? To at least deter criminals, or catch them in the act."

"Good luck getting Sully to fork out for it." Greg rumbled.

"He'd up our rent." Spencer agreed.

Goldie chewed on her lip. "I need my rent to stay the same right now. Do we have to choose between having a home and being safe?"

"No," Greg said calmly, "That's why we're having the meetings. To make sure we're looking out for one another. You know, noticing anyone strange around."

Goldie nodded, but she still looked shaken. "Well, thanks for telling us anyway. How many people are coming?"

Greg shrugged as he started back down the hallway to the staircase. "Not sure. Angela's already spoken to some of the other tenants. That Rachel Ellis woman is definitely coming. It's tomorrow night at nine, at Angela's bookstore. See ya there." Greg raised a hand in parting as he walked back down the stairs.

Just as Goldie opened her mouth to say something to Spencer and Alex, the sound of footsteps echoed up the stairwell and down the hallway.

They could hear Greg greet the newcomer and seconds later, a woman, in a floral shirt, black pants and high-heels tottered up the stairs. She was short and busty, with dark hair that curled gently around her face. The make-up she wore was understated and carefully applied. She was older than the three of them, perhaps in her late forties. In her manicured hands, she was holding a pile of leaflets.

When she saw the three of them, her dark eyes became wide and inquisitive as she trotted towards them, her heels clicking along the floor.

"Ah, good." The woman sang. She lifted the leaflets in her hands and started handing them out. Angie gave one to Spencer, Goldie and Alex. "These are about the meeting for the tenants of *Cassandra's*." She clarified. "Greg said he told you, yes?"

Everyone nodded as they looked down at their leaflet.

The woman's eyes settled on Alex and looked at her expectantly. She smiled and held out her hand. "I'm Angela Quinn. Everyone calls me Angie. I live in apartment 32. And you?"

Alex gave her another brittle smile. It felt like that was all she did since she got to Kenzo. "Alex."

"Uh, Alex who?" Angie prodded.

"Alexandria Raffaello."

"Oh," Angie sighed. "And have you just moved in?"

"Yeah, into apartment 14."

Angie's eyes lit up. "Oh, so, I'm sure you'll have lots of questions for us, then."

Alex shook her head. "Not really." She pressed her tongue to the roof of her mouth as she tried to remain even-tempered. She returned her attention to the leaflet. As Angie had said, it was advertising a meeting for the residents of *Cassandra's Palace* in a local bookstore named *The Book Corner* tomorrow night at 9 pm.

"So, I'll see you there at 9 pm, at my bookstore." She leaned towards Alex and placed a hand on her arm. "It's just down the road. It'll be a great place to talk about the issues we wanted to address with Mr Sullivan. All the residents will have a chance to air their grievances. You'll be coming, right?"

Alex shook her head. "I don't think I'll be able to make it," Alex said apologetically. "I'm still moving in and I've gotta get the place cleaned."

Angie pouted. "You'll still have time for us. It won't take long."

Alex gritted her teeth. "I can't."

Angie pouted. She wasn't ready to give up, but Alex was adamant. "I'll see." She lied. "Nice to meet you all, but I gotta put my shopping in the fridge. See you."

Alex edged away from the group and ducked back into her apartment.

She shut the door gently and took a big step back from the door, sighing. A few moments later, she heard the three of them part ways.

While Alex had been vague on purpose when she had insisted that she had things to do, she was telling the truth. She had plans to clean her apartment, put away her groceries, to cook, and it was already half past three. Even if everything went well, she'd still spend the rest of the day cleaning and there were other things she had to take care of. She'd be too tired tomorrow to plaster on a smile, especially if the other residents grilled her the way Angie had.

She dropped her keys back into her backpack, shrugged off her coat, and left it by the couch before she began unpacking the bags. She sifted through the groceries. Some of the frozen food had started to defrost. She picked them up and shoved everything that needed to remain cold haphazardly in the fridge, and put everything else that was edible in the empty cupboards.

Next, she gathered her cleaning supplies and dumped them on the table.

While out shopping, she had bought a sponge, a bucket, a dustpan and a brush, a small kettle and a pot with cutlery. She would get the rest later.

She started by picking up half of the cleaning supplies she had bought, the bucket and a sponge before she marched into the bathroom.

Alex didn't stop until the floor, sink and bath were gleaming in the dull light filtering in from the window, and the walls were drenched in the distinct lemony scent that was attached to the cleaner she had used.

Next, she moved on to her kitchen, scrubbing the cabinets, the counters and the refrigerator.

She dusted her apartment from top to bottom, even taking the time to polish the tables. She vacuumed the floor, and couch, before taking her sponge and bucket filled with disinfectant on a tour of her bedroom, bathroom, living area and kitchen.

When she had finished cleaning, she changed the sheets on her bed to one of the ones she had just bought. She then put up the curtains for each of the windows she had counted.

Alex had convinced herself to buy utensils, a pot and a metal kettle, so she took those out. Then she began taking out her small set of plates, bowls, cups and utensils. They were all plastic, so she didn't worry too much about throwing them down on the table. Everything outside of her bag was replaceable. It made no sense to buy expensive things she might have to leave behind.

She checked the receipt before tossing it back into the bag. She'd never experienced the luxury of shopping for shopping's sake, but these were things that she needed.

When she was done unpacking kitchen items, she went back to the shopping bags that were left. She put everything away except for a packet of noodles.

She boiled the water in her new kettle, poured some into a cup with the noodles, took a fork and her dinner, and sat on the edge of the couch to eat. As she slurped down the last of the spicy noodles, she listened to the street noises drifting in through her window, and her thoughts returned to the meeting tomorrow.

Even when faced with the intrusive neighbours she had met in the last few days, she enjoyed the mundane tasks her new apartment brought her. Every small thing she did helped to make it her home.

The apartment hadn't been too difficult to clean. The job had just seemed bigger from the other side of it.

Honestly, the more she thought about it, the more she realised she really wouldn't be too tired tomorrow for Angie's meeting.

While she did think it would be better for her to lie low, it would be even more to her benefit to know what was going on. And considering the way Angie acted, as if her word was law, her absence would probably land her on the wrong foot with Angie and draw too much attention.

As much as she wanted to remain out of it, she didn't have much of a choice.

But, while unpleasant, it wasn't anything she couldn't handle. She had spent just over an hour scrubbing the floors, so a short meeting would be cake.

This was her new home, and she would do what she needed to keep it.

CHAPTER 8

When Alex stepped out of her apartment the next evening, she was swallowed almost immediately by the darkness that filled the empty hallway. The one frosted window at the end of the hall was the only source of light that allowed her to see her feet and not much else.

As she shut the door behind her, the dull light that had filtered out of her apartment behind her was extinguished. She took care to lock the door and tested the doorknob with a shake for good measure. When it resisted her, she turned and headed for the stairwell.

The lights that lined the walls of the stairs remained dormant and dull. By the time she had reached the ground floor, she was glad that even though it was after 8 pm, there was still enough light filtering in from the outside to give her some indication of her surroundings.

As she walked she felt the air around her grow heavier as she stepped out of the stairwell on the ground floor, and through the corridor that led to the main entrance.

As she passed the second apartment door on her left, she felt a shiver pass down her spine and the hair on the back of her neck raised.

Alone in the hallway, she felt like she was being watched by someone she couldn't see. Alex picked up her pace as she crossed the main entrance and slipped out of the front door into the evening chill.

It didn't take her long to find the store that was mentioned in the letter. It was quite close to *The Palace*.

The other buildings around it had crumbled and aged, but Angela Quinn's bookstore remained, happily tucked away between two derelict buildings, without care. Golden light flooded out of the windows as it stood, like a beacon in the dark.

The bell above the door tinkled as Alex pushed it open and stepped inside. The warmth and the strong musk of the bookstore enveloped her as her eyes adjusted from the dim, blinding darkness that had covered her eyes, to the bright golden glow that saturated everything it touched. As she moved inside, a low chatter drifted out to greet her.

The interior of the bookstore was larger than the outside suggested. There were tall rows of bookshelves that lined the back and front of the store, but still, at the core, there was a large expanse of the store that was left for the customers, and it was here where many of the residents of *Cassandra's Palace* had already gathered. Mismatched chairs had been set out in a semblance of a circle, allowing everyone to see and interact with one another.

It was only while she was staring at the table that had been covered with refreshments and snacks that it became clear that this meeting was being taken far more seriously than she had initially thought.

She had pictured a few people gathered, talking about their inconveniences for fifteen minutes, before they all went their separate ways, until the next month.

The residents were all different ages, but they all spoke to each other freely, with familiarity. These people knew each other as more than just brief acquaintances. They spoke to each other regularly. They most likely shared details of their lives. And they would expect Alex to do the same.

As she watched, Alex spotted Goldie and Spencer sitting with two older women and an older man, laughing at something the man had said. Greg was in the back, in conversation with another man. Other people were speaking to the people next to them, while a tall man spoke more generally to the rest of the group.

Alex wasn't sure what they were discussing, but it was painfully clear that, yes, they were all familiar with one another.

As she stepped towards the group, she was spotted.

Slowly, as they all began to notice her, they turned to her curiously, their conversations dying down almost immediately.

Once Goldie spotted her, she raised her hand and waved her over.

"Is this the meeting?" Alex asked them in greeting. Alex knew it was, but it was enough to tell them what she was doing there.

The tall man that had been speaking to the group leaned forward in his seat. Like many of the others, he looked to be in his forties. His hair was cut close to his head and neat. He wore a plain dark green sweater and slacks. "You're a resident of *Cassandra's Palace?*" He asked carefully as if he was afraid of confusing her.

"That's Alex, Nate. She's one of us." Goldie explained. "She's here for the meeting."

Nate looked from Goldie to Alex. "Really?"

Alex nodded. "I just moved in the day before yesterday."

The man nodded once in acknowledgement and rose from his seat, extending his hand towards her. "I'm Nate Russell."

Alex walked forward and took his hand. "Alexandria Raffaello." She offered.

As they separated, Angela Quinn tottered from around a bookshelf at the back of the store to join the group.

When she saw Alex, she beamed. "Oh, I'm so glad you could make it. Sit, sit." She ushered Alex over to an empty seat next to her own, and with that, she began the meeting.

"Everyone, this is Alex. She just moved into number 14 this week, so this is her first meeting."

Alex felt her cheeks burn at the attention, and she lowered her head in embarrassment, as the other residents offered up their welcomes.

She smiled bashfully at each one, but she was grateful when their attention was taken away from her and drawn to the reason why the meeting had been called.

Alex listened carefully, as Angela began explaining to the group why they were all there. Most of it was probably for Alex's benefit, but everyone listened patiently.

This was a meeting that they tried to have at least once a month, to discuss issues they had with *Cassandra's Palace* so that they could note them down and then take their issues to Vincent Sullivan. Or as they, not-so-affectionately called him, Sully. Since they all had trouble tracking him individually, they decided this was the best way to get their concerns to him.

But, it didn't seem to be working. Sully remained elusive and unhelpful.

Still, they all aired their grievances, one at a time. Broken boilers, warped windows and fickle fuses. Alex didn't have anything to add, but they all assured her that in time she would.

Angela took down detailed notes of what was said. She promised to give them to Sully, but Alex was sure that they would go missing somewhere between Angela sliding the envelope under his door, and Sully opening it.

It was close to 10 pm when their discussion turned towards other concerns. Not as immediate, but still as concerning. It was the arrival of a new person, that changed the course of the conversation.

The bell over the door rang and after a few seconds, a voice drifted in through the shop. "Hello? Angie? It's Rachel."

Angie looked up in surprise before she tottered to the aisle. "Down here, Rachel!" She called out.

Soft, sure footsteps marched down the wooden panel floor, and a second later, a familiar blonde woman turned the corner.

Rachel was well-dressed, in a blazer and light, floral shirt, with her handbag in the crook of her arm, as if she had only stopped off at the meeting on her way to somewhere much nicer.

"Hello everyone." Rachel Ellis announced in a clear, authoritative voice. She didn't need to raise her voice higher than her normal speaking level for her voice to carry across the room. Some murmured back their greetings, but a few ignored her. Rachel, however, didn't appear to notice.

Rachel looked around at the faces of the residents, and her pale eyes landed on Alex. They narrowed for a second before she smiled. "Hello again. I'm not sure if you remember me from a few nights ago."

Alex grimaced. "I do." She mumbled.

"Great." Rachel nodded. She looked around. "What brings you here?"

All eyes in the room moved from Rachel to Alex. She shrugged. "I just moved into *Cassandra's Palace*." She repeated. "I'm here for the meeting."

Rachel's eyes sharpened. She tilted her head to the side. "Into apartment 14? So soon?"

"What's wrong with that?"

Rachel frowned at her, her eyes probing. "You've moved into apartment 14, right? Elise Chambers' apartment, isn't it? I wasn't aware it was on the market."

Rachel's voice was light and casual, but her eyes were fixed on Alex. They sent a chill down Alex's spine and she knew that Rachel was searching for something, but Alex honestly didn't know what. Since she hadn't known what had happened before she had rented the apartment, she couldn't see any significance to it. But then, she wasn't a reporter.

Rachel smiled again and her eyes softened, but the chill remained. "I'm sorry. Has no one told you about the last tenant?"

"I didn't hear anything about that until I got here."

"Really? Vincent Sullivan didn't tell you?"

From across the room, Alex saw Spencer shift in his seat irritably. "I thought you were busy looking into Marcia's missing kid." Spencer snapped. "Didn't know you were looking into Elise too."

Rachel raised her head to glare at him. "I am."

Spencer crossed his arms over his chest, glaring right back. "Well, maybe you should focus on that first."

There was a heavy silence in the room as Rachel and Spencer exchanged non-verbal blows.

"What about Elise?" The large grizzled man named Mike asked. "You work with the police, don't you, Spence? How come the police don't know where Marie went? And how come they can't catch a simple animal running around Kenzo?" His eyes were now fixed on Spencer. "Detective Lovett and Li are no better than Sully."

"It's not as simple as that," Spencer argued. "Marie is *not* considered a missing person. To the police at least. She left a note. Besides, they're homicide detectives. It's an entirely different department that deals with missing people and a completely different set of people to deal with dangerous animals. They catch human criminals, not animals. And they certainly aren't family therapists."

Despite the reasonable response Spencer offered, his words did nothing to soothe a disgruntled audience.

"What about the animal that killed Elise? They don't seem to be catching that one. Is it really a bear, like the others? You work at the morgue, don't you?" Mike asked. "Why can't you tell us what you know?"

The attention of the room rested on him, and Spencer shifted under its weight. "I can't."

"We understand you're in a difficult position, Spencer," Angela offered sympathetically. "It's okay."

"No, it's not." Mike snapped. "We deserve to know."

"I can't," Spencer repeated.

"Spencer has a point-" Rachel interjected.

"Because it's confidential?" Mike spat back. "Who cares, if it keeps someone else from being attacked?"

Spencer lowered his head and ground his teeth together. "Even still...I can't." He muttered.

"Come on, Spence." Goldie prodded. Dozens of pairs of eyes watched Spencer intently, waiting for him to break.

They waited hungrily for any scrap of information, so eager that they were ready to eat the person who could give it to them.

Spencer clasped his hands together on his lap as his mouth formed a thin line. "I'm sorry."

The expectant crowd sat back in their seats with grumbles of disappointment, annoyance and even disapproval. They rippled with unused energy. "So you won't tell us to save your own skin?" An older woman named Claire asked. "For your job?" The others hummed in agreement.

"I can't tell you, because we don't know."

There was a tense silence where everyone waited for more and even Alex, who had been trying her best to turn herself invisible for the entire meeting, leaned forward in her seat.

"What do you mean?" Goldie asked.

Spencer's shoulders slumped. "We can't find any trace of the animal. We've...we've been working with specialists and none of them has any clues about what kind of animal could do the damage this one has."

Angela scoffed in disbelief. "*None* of you have any idea? How? How is that even possible?"

Spencer met her eyes. "There's no animal they're aware of that is physically able to do what it's done, to move around without leaving a trail, or droppings or a nest."

The group rustled, as they looked to each other for clarity, but everyone looked as puzzled as the person beside them.

"So, it's a human, then? It's murder?" Goldie asked, looking around the group for confirmation.

Spencer shrugged. "Whatever is responsible seems smart, like a human." he offered, "but a human couldn't be behind this either. There are teeth and claw marks."

"So a human with a dog, then," Nate asked. "He uses a dog to kill them."

Goldie shook her head. "But that means that this wasn't a wrong-place-wrong-time thing. Those people were murdered!"

Spencer shook his head and rubbed his eyes under his glasses. "Or it could simply mean that she was killed, and a bear found her body."

Before anyone could say anything else, the bell over the front door rang, and everyone looked up.

"That should be the detectives," Angela said as she stood up from her seat. "I invited them to come by."

Alex shifted back in her seat, surprised that she had been teetering on the edge of it. "For Sully? Are things that serious?"

Angie pursed her lips. "I wanted to get them involved in beefing up our security. Get some suggestions about-" The phone rang. "Oh, could you go meet them?" She asked Alex, trotting off to the back of the shop.

Reluctantly, Alex got up from her seat as the residents started talking to each other about what they had found out. She followed the path through the bookshelves back to the front of the store. Heavy thuds of boots hit the floorboards ahead and the low chatter of two men reached her ears. She had already reached the bookshelves at the front of the store before anyone else had even moved.

As she got closer, the low thrum of the two voices became familiar. Alex reached the front of the store and saw Detective Henry Lovett and Detective David Li.

Detective Lovett spotted her first and scowled at her over Detective Li's shoulder. Detective Li turned and frowned at her in surprise. "I didn't expect to see you here." He admitted.

Alex wanted to say the same. "You're here for the meeting, aren't you?"

Detective Li nodded, glancing back at his stony-faced partner. "Angie asked us to stop by. Where is she?"

Alex pointed behind her. "Answering the phone."

Detective Lovett cleared his throat. "While you're here, we've been meaning to talk to you, too. What are you doing here?"

"I'm here for the meeting." Alex pointed at one of Angela's flyers stuck to the end of a bookshelf. I just moved in. Why do you want to talk to me?" Alex asked warily.

"You moved into *Cassandra's Palace?*" He growled.

"Yeah." Alex frowned at the two of them. "Is there something wrong?"

The detectives exchanged a look before Detective Lovett continued. "As I said, we had a few questions to ask you. Can we talk?"

"Sure." Alex wanted to ask how they managed to end up at the one place she would be, but instead, she pressed her tongue to the roof of her mouth.

"We found some remains near the bus stop where we found you."

The words didn't register at first. They meant nothing to her as she turned them over in her head. She blinked, and Detective Lovett elaborated. "We found partial human remains buried in the woods by the bus stop."

"*Remains?*"

The three of them turned to see that Angela and Spencer had followed Alex and heard the tail end of their conversation. Angie stepped forwards, and her voice rose in pitch. "What are you talking about?"

Detective Lovett nodded to Angela. "Evenin', Angie. We're in the middle of an investigation."

"You're always in the middle of an investigation." She snapped. "When are you gonna reach the end of one? That's what I want to know!"

The two men remained silent and turned their attention to Spencer, at the annoyance of Angela. Detective Li nodded to Spencer. "We'll need you to get to the morgue and see what you can find. We need to know who the remains belong to."

Spencer gave them a sharp nod. He looked down at Alex. "You found it?" Angela's keen eyes snapped to her.

Alex shook her head. "I didn't."

"No, we did," Detective Lovett admitted. "It was half an hour away from the last incident. Alex was waiting for a bus nearby when we found her. We just thought we should let her know." His eyes met Alex's. "Can we talk in private?"

"Wait!" Spencer held up his hand. He turned to Alex. "You were there? Did you see anything? Anyone?"

Detective Li stepped forwards and herded Alex to Detective Lovett and the front door. When she was close enough, Detective Lovett guided her to the door.

"We'll let you know later, Spence," Detective Li promised as he backed away. "But right now we need you down at the morgue." The tinkle of the bell rang out and Alex was led back out onto the street. As the door closed behind Detective Li, she could see that the other residents had joined Angela and Spencer at the front of the door.

Detective Lovett and Detective Li led Alex away from the warmth and the scrutiny of Angela Quinn's bookstore. When they were at least a few buildings away, they both stopped and turned to her.

"Have you read the newspaper today?" Detective Li asked suddenly.

"No, I didn't leave my apartment 'til just now to come here." Alex shrugged her shoulders and shivered where she stood. She was suddenly brought back to the night before last when she met them. She had thought that had been the end of it.

"Thought you would've been more invested." Detective Li mused.

Alex met his eyes steadily and shrugged. "I just figured I was lucky to meet you guys and then moved on. It's best to leave stuff like that to the professionals, right?"

Detective Lovett hummed. "Yeah. Have you had contact with Marcia Rosen?" Detective Lovett asked suddenly, his sharp eyes narrowed on her.

"Yeah, I met her the same night I met you. You were there."

Detective Li nodded. "And the day after, you had an altercation with her in a supermarket."

Alex nodded numbly. "Yeah, she grabbed me, and I told her to leave me alone. What- I'm sorry, but what is this about?"

Both men exchanged looks again. Finally, Detective Lovett spoke. "Marcia Rosen was found dead in her home in Belamour."

Alex stared at Detective Lovett for a moment, but all she could see was Marcia's blotchy face as Alex shouted at her in the middle of the aisle. "I-I...I don't...what happened?" She wanted to hear the words out loud, to confirm what she already knew.

"We think she was murdered. A few blows to the head."

Alex exhaled heavily. Of course, two homicide detectives wouldn't drop by just to tell her that a woman she barely knew died from natural causes, but a small part of her had hoped that they were just making conversation.

But this wasn't a friendly visit between two policemen and a civilian. This was an interrogation between two policemen and a suspect.

Alex tried to swallow, but her dry throat resisted her. "I did argue with her. Publicly." She muttered hoarsely.

She opened her mouth and once she began to talk, she found that she couldn't stop. "I was shopping for groceries and she saw me. Rachel, er..the reporter lady that was with her that night, said something to her and then she...Marcia decided that I must know something about her daughter, or the two of you. I told her I didn't and when I tried to leave, she grabbed me, so I grabbed her and told her to back off. She had a friend with her, Nicolette...something. She heard everything. The last time I saw Marcia, she left with Nicolette. I paid for my stuff and went to buy some more stuff in a furniture store and then went home. I met

Goldie when I came in. She saw me." She pointed back towards the bookstore. "I didn't leave my apartment after that."

Both detectives nodded at her explanation. "That lines up with what we've heard."

Alex exhaled slowly. "Ok. But what about Rachel? She didn't mention anything."

"She doesn't know. We haven't told her." Detective Li crossed his arms over his chest. "We've tried to keep this as...confidential as possible, to not impede the investigation."

Meaning, they didn't want Rachel to write an article before they had even begun the investigation.

Detective Lovett fished into his pocket and pulled out a photo. He held it out to her. "Do you know him? Ever seen him before?"

Alex looked down at the picture. It was a headshot of a man in an expensive suit, with a narrow, pointed face. His hair was dark and his eyes honey brown.

She shook her head. "No. Why?"

"He's been missing for a few days. We just wanted to see if you'd seen him around.'

"Does he have something to do with this? Is he a suspect? You know, for the remains? Or the other incident." Alex looked between the two men.

They shared another look between them, one that told Alex more than they wanted it to.

"He's missing. He's from Belamour." David explained. "We were just checking."

"How long has he been missing?"

"A week." He answered automatically.

"But I only got here the day before yesterday. How would I have seen him if I just got into Kenzo? I haven't even been over there. The closest I got was Brewster."

Neither man answered her, but Alex didn't need her question answered. Whoever he was, they thought that Alex might have seen him the night before. But why? He didn't look like the type that would hang around in the woods, murderer or not.

They only asked her a few more questions, and by the time they had finished, the residents of *Cassandra's* were already milling around outside, hoping to overhear. Rachel lurked nearby, watching the three of them with open curiosity.

Detective Lovett eyed the crowd cautiously, his eyes lingering on Rachel before he turned back to her. "So you'll be sticking around Troye, then?"

Alex nodded. "That's the plan.

"But, apart from everything else, you settled in ok?" He questioned, conversationally.

Alex gave him a curt nod. "Yes."

Detective Lovett looked up at the bookstore behind her. "And you found everything, okay? Are you good?"

Alex nodded again and gave him a bright smile that didn't move the upper part of her face. She truly was grateful, but she couldn't help but wonder if these questions would backfire on her eventually.

She didn't need cops sniffing around her, asking questions about her and where she came from, or her past address and details. If they forced her to tell them, he might start asking more questions.

Such as why did she move from place to place frequently, where's your family, or what kind of name is 'Raffaello' anyway, because she honestly didn't know.

The man she had gotten it from seemed to like it well enough.

Looking up at the two of them, she could see that they were checking her over. She didn't need him and Detective Li to get more invested in her.

All Alex wanted was just to blend in.

That was all.

"I'm sorry that I couldn't be more helpful." She shrugged again, taking a small step back until a thought crossed her mind and stopped her retreat. "Do you think it was connected to the other incident, now?"

Detective Lovett rubbed at his chin and shrugged. "Don't know, still too soon to tell. But if you remember anything else, or see anything, let us know." He handed her a card.

As she took it, she realised just how small her hand was in comparison to his. Compared to his, her fingers were like small brittle twigs next to branches. She looked down at the scribbled note. Both Detective Lovett's and Detective Li's numbers had been scratched into it.

Detective Li pointed at the card. "If you can't call one of us, call the other. One of us will pick up."

Alex nodded again. "Thanks." She sighed in relief.

"Well, if there's anything you need." He said as they turned to leave.

Out of nowhere, another thought popped into her head, and she called out to him. "Uhm, Detectives?"

They turned back to face her. Detective Lovett raised a heavy brow. "Yeah?"

"Do you know any other supermarkets?"

Detective Li scoffed and the corners of Detective Lovett's mouth tilted upwards and his brows raised, scratching at his jaw. "You haven't had a chance to explore your new neighbourhood?"

Reluctantly, Alex shrugged. "Just a bit."

"Any different from Oakland?"

Alex shrugged noncommittally, still determined to ease herself from the conversation. "A bit, I guess. But, I like it better here. More to explore, you know?"

This time, Detective Lovett looked puzzled. "Most people don't feel that way. They see run-down blocks and not much else." He added.

Alex shrugged, looking around at the cracked pavement under her shoes. "I can see that. But I'm not fussy. I've been in worse places."

He scratched his ear. "Well, how about your job?"

Alex looked around for inspiration, but found none on the pavement and shrugged again. "I don't have one yet. I'm gonna look for something." She said vaguely.

"If you're interested, there's a coffee shop in Rossum, called *The Hideaway*. I know the owner. I just spoke to him this morning. He's looking for someone reliable. I can talk to him for ya."

He reached inside his jacket and pulled out a small pad and a pen. He scribbled down the address and phone number on the pad, ripped the page off and handed it to her.

Alex took it, her eyes skimming over the details and she smiled again. "Sure. Thanks."

"Alright, see ya." The two of them turned and sauntered back to Detective Lovett's truck and climbed in. The truck's engine roared to life before he and Detective Li drove away from the curb. As they passed, Detective Li waved in her direction and she returned it.

With a heavy sigh of relief, Alex looked down at the card one more time and slid it into her pocket, along with the paper.

One of the many things she had to do was to search for a job nearby. If she got the job at the coffee shop...well, then that was just another thing off one of her many lists.

Under the heavy glare of the people who were now her very vigilant and invested neighbours, Alex turned and sped back to her apartment, ignoring the whispers as she went.

CHAPTER 9

When Alex returned to her apartment, her first instinct was to pack her bag with everything new she had bought, to pack up all the food in her cupboards and just move again. She knew she hadn't been responsible for the death of Marcia Rosen, but she couldn't afford an investigation into her background. She had no ID and no history to speak of that would leave a trace on any database. That would raise suspicion and a mountain of questions that she couldn't answer.

Alex stood inside the mouth of her apartment and looked around. She had hoped this would become a home to her, somewhere she could rest.

She exhaled heavily as she threw her bag down. She didn't want to leave and probably wasn't smart to go anyway.

Detective Henry Lovett had offered her a job, so it didn't seem as if he believed her to be responsible for any murder.

Perhaps, if she just remained where she was, lying low, then perhaps it won't even come to the formal investigation. She sighed again and began to take off her clothes and headed to the bathroom for a shower.

While Alex had been shaken from her eventful past few days, she decided to push through. She didn't want to leave again when she had already put so much effort into cleaning her apartment. Leaving would mean that she would find somewhere else to live with even less money than she had now. Not to mention, it would make her look extremely guilty.

She had nothing to do with Marcia's death or anyone else's in Kenzo, so there was no reason to worry.

The next morning, she made her decision. She wouldn't leave, but she would wait it out and see what happened next. She would take Henry up on his offer and get the job. That way, she'd have more money than she currently had to work with.

It was still in the early hours of the morning when Alex woke up a few days after the meeting. She had a shower and got dressed before it was even light outside. She didn't bother to grab breakfast, instead, she just grabbed her bag and left her apartment.

She stepped out onto the pavement in front of *Cassandra's Palace* and shoved her hands into her pockets.

It took her just over forty-five minutes to find *The Hideaway*. She had walked from Troye to Rossum, something that was much easier during the day and far less terrifying.

There had been a definite improvement in the local environment as she left Troye and entered Rossum, but in Alex's opinion, you were just as likely to be robbed here as you were down the street.

The Hideaway was a large coffee shop, with most of the front of the building built with thick, tinted glass and a giant sign on the side of the building, naming it *The Hideaway*, with fancy graphics decorating it.

Inside the coffee shop were thick wooden tables and chairs. On the other side of the room was a counter with displays of food. Behind the counter was the area reserved for staff, with various coffee machines along the wall.

As she pushed open the door, a loud bell chimed, announcing her entrance. The light from overhead was dimmer but warm and inviting, and the smell of coffee swarmed her. She let the door close behind her and walked further in.

Sat at one of the tables in front of the counter was a tall bronze-haired man, reading a newspaper. Next to him, a lanky dark-haired man in a plaid shirt rose from his seat. "Gotta go. See ya." He said to the other man. He nodded to Alex as he passed her.

"Later." The man with the newspaper called behind his friend.

The man sitting in front of her was older than Alex, by at least a decade, in his late thirties. His thick, dark bronze hair brushed the back of his neck, reaching down towards the tops of his shoulders. Though his head was tilted down, with his attention focused intently on the newspaper under his nose, Alex could see that he had a sharp, angular jaw and a nose to match.

His long legs were stretched out lazily in front of him, with his legs crossed at the ankles. Slowly, he flicked through the pages with practised ease. His navy shirt was rolled at the sleeves and his dark jeans covered his work boots. A small, maroon apron, embroidered with the logo of the store dangled from his pocket.

Alex stepped forward and cleared her throat. "Erm, hi?"

"You need somethin', sweetheart?" The man drawled lazily. "Really hope you don't, 'cause I'm on my break."

Alex raised an eyebrow at the man as he flicked through another page. She reached into her pocket and fished through for the note Detective Lovett gave her. "Are you...Reggie Price?"

The man chuckled darkly. "Hell, no."

"Well, I'm looking for him."

"To complain?"

"No, about a job."

Finally, the man raised his head an inch above the paper in his hands. "About my job?"

Alex shook her head. "No." She paused, "At least, I don't think so. I was just told that the owner of the store was looking for someone to hire."

"And who told you that?"

"A friend." She answered vaguely.

"A friend." He repeated softly.

"Yep."

The man uncrossed his legs and shifted his weight back onto his feet, but he didn't rise from his seat. His dark brows lowered over his piercing blue eyes, as he stared up at her.

"Some friend you got there. You sure he's your friend? Doesn't seem to have a name."

Alex folded her arms over her chest, raising herself to her full height. Not that it increased by much. "A man named Henry Lovett told me about it. *Detective* Lovett. He's the one who suggested the job."

Any trace of humour on the man's face was wiped from his expression completely. He closed his eyes and inhaled deeply through his nose. "That bastard!" He muttered under his breath. His eyes snapped back open and, he glared up at her, his eyes burning. "So, what? My brother sent you, then?"

Brother?

"Uhm...what?"

The man rolled his eyes. "You said my brother told you about the job?"

"Well, I didn't know..." She trailed off. "He's your...?"

"Yeah." The man muttered, wiping his jaw with a rough hand. "Bastard always said Reggie could do better and just get someone else. Didn't think he'd actually do anything about it."

Just as Alex opened her mouth to apologise, the back door, labelled 'employees only', opened and out walked a small, round and balding man with brown skin. He looked between her and the other man, and for a second, a flicker of annoyance flashed over his face before it smoothed out into a pleasant smile. Behind him trailed a girl around Alex's age, with short brown hair, wearing an apron. Her eyes narrowed as they landed on the man sitting in front of Alex before she went back out through the door she had just entered.

"Everything ok?" The man chirped, as he glared at the man by the counter. "Frank doing his job?" It was said to sound like a joke, but there was no humour in the smaller man's voice. The girl who had just left, burst back into the room and scowled in the direction of 'Frank' before leaving again, but he paid neither of them any attention.

"Apparently, Henry told her about you looking for someone to replace me." The man named Frank muttered.

The man brightened instantly and he scurried forwards, around the counter. "Ah, Alex, isn't it? Henry told me you're new in town, looking for a job?"

Alex frowned in confusion. "Yeah, I just talked to him and-"

"You're hired!"

Alex looked from the small man to Frank, who scoffed. "Really?" She asked slowly. "But...you don't have any questions for me?"

The man shrugged. "You need a job, I need an employee that actually does work. It's not like it's a difficult job. And if Henry recommended you, that must mean something. I guess he likes you."

Detective Lovett hadn't given her any indication that he had any substantial positive feelings towards her that would make him have faith in her, but if Reggie wanted to think that, Alex didn't see any reason to try and persuade him otherwise.

The small man held out his hand. Alex took it and he shook it with all the enthusiasm he could muster. "I'm Reggie Price, the proud owner of the best coffee shop in all of Kenzo-"

Frank scoffed loudly, and Reggie glared at him.

Reggie jerked his head towards him. "And that is the biggest tool this side of Kenzo, Frank Lovett. Only has this job 'cause I owe his brother, Henry. And you really don't want to piss off a cop."

He let go of Alex's hand, only to wrap his thick arm around her shoulders to drag her forward.

For the next ten minutes, Reggie babbled on and on about the details and perks of the job. Alex tried to pay close attention to everything he said, but her mind pushed out the chatter when he went off on a tangent, which happened more often than not.

"It's $4.50 an hour, and you'll be working with Lisa- you just met her, she's another employee that works here- on Tuesdays and Thursdays, and with Frank on Wednesdays and Fridays. Oh, and-"

He ran to the back of the store and came back with a uniform and an apron. He held it up for Alex to inspect.

"This is the uniform that you'll be wearing, But, since Frank doesn't even bother, just make sure you at least wear the apron, okay?"

Reggie barely stopped to breathe, let alone for her to talk. She just kept nodding.

Surprisingly, Reggie already knew a lot about her. According to him, it was information that Henry had told him between her conversation with Henry and her arriving at *The Hideaway*. She hadn't realised that Detective Lovett had paid that much attention to her. She tried to brush the knowledge aside, but a small voice of doubt and fear that lurked at the back of her head wondered if he had an ulterior motive for getting her the job.

Perhaps, the offer wasn't as altruistic as Reggie made it out to be.

Perhaps, this was a way of keeping an eye on her.

But as she watched Reggie whisking around the counter, showing her everything like an excited child, she couldn't help but doubt that idea.

Reggie wasn't the best person to use for spying. A guarded man like Detective Lovett would never use someone like Reggie.

She was overthinking the situation again, and it was making her paranoid.

But as her eyes drifted from Reggie to Frank, a question struck her.

Henry wouldn't use Reggie, but would he use Frank?

Clearly, there were a few issues between them, but they were brothers. For all she knew, this was just an insignificant sibling rivalry, one easily brushed away for more important things.

But it wasn't like she was guilty of anything, anyway. So, she had nothing to fear.

Not in Kenzo, anyway. Not from the detectives.

As she looked up, she realised that Frank was now watching her with the same intensity his brother had, just as Reggie came to the end of his speech.

She hadn't seen the resemblance between the two initially, but now that she looked at Frank, she saw that while their eyes and their hair were very different colours, their eyes were the same shape. Both shrewd and penetrating.

Frank was wirier while Henry was broad, but both of them were around six feet. Their faces were both sharp, but while Henry's jaw was more square, Frank's was more angular. Henry was probably in his late forties, or early fifties and Frank was younger. There weren't any streaks of grey in his hair, but his hair was considerably lighter than Henry's, so the grey wouldn't be as obvious.

"So, any questions?" Reggie asked hopefully, rocking backwards and forwards on his feet.

Alex shook her head. "No, I'm good, thanks."

Reggie beamed, as a phone rang. "Damn, well, I'll see you next week, then. Take care."

With that, he rushed to the back room, leaving her with Frank.

There was an uncomfortable silence between the two of them, as they both sized the other up.

"So, how did you meet him? Henry?" Frank asked finally. "Because I haven't seen you around before."

"I just moved into Troye a few days ago. I was waiting at a bus stop when Detective Lovett and Detective Li were driving by. The road had been shut down because of an incident and so they decided to help me out. They gave me a lift."

"Ok." Frank dragged his hand through his stubble, his blue eyes pinning her where she stood. He frowned down at the newspaper in front of him. "Wait, where did you meet them?"

"At a bus stop just inside of Rossum."

"So, near where...?" he gestured to the discarded newspaper on the counter next to him. It was only then that Alex took a proper look at the front page of the newspaper Frank had been reading. The headline read 'KENZO'S MONSTER ATTACKS AGAIN' above a picture of a crime scene that was teeming with police investigators.

Alex shrugged. "I guess. I'm not familiar with the area, but Detective...Uhm, Henry, said that there was an incident nearby. He didn't give me any details about it, though."

Frank hummed thoughtfully. "Well, can't tell what they don't know. The police haven't been able to track this thing down for months. Don't even know what's been attacking people. Some think it's a rabid animal, like a bear, or something others think it might be a serial killer covering his tracks. Some fellas I know, down at the bar think both, after a few drinks."

"Yeah, but no one knows for sure, do they?" She mused. "Weren't there confirmed bear attacks?"

"Police said it was. Journalists say otherwise. You haven't heard about this before?"

Alex shook her head.

Frank raised his eyebrows. "You moved to a place, and you never checked to see if it hit the headlines?"

Alex scowled down at her shoes. "I didn't hear anything about this."

"You don't watch TV? Or talk to people?"

Alex's scowl deepened. "No."

Frank shook his head in disbelief. "Then you really are lucky that you bumped into Henry and David." He picked up the newspaper and handed it to her. "But between you and me, I don't think it's much to worry about. Just stay out of the woods."

She took the newspaper from his hands and looked over the front page more closely. It said exactly what Frank had just told her, no more, no less.

The succinct summary should have cleared things up for her, but all it did was give her more questions to ponder over. "So, that's why Animal Control is involved? To identify the creature? Or to track it?" Alex doubted that whatever was in the woods would let anyone see it if it was smart enough, but information about how it worked might help.

"Yeah, they would be the ones who know how to track a dangerous animal. Nothing for us to worry about, I'm sure," Frank announced cheerfully. He leaned over the counter, grabbed a pack of cigarettes, and then grabbed his coat.

He nodded to her as he walked past her, and all the tables, to the main doors. "Come on, then."

Alex turned to face him but stayed where she stood. "What?"

Frank gave her a toothy grin, "I'll drop you off home. I'm knocking off early. Least I can do."

Alex glanced at the clock on the wall behind Frank. It wasn't even 1 o'clock yet.

She was starting to see why Reggie had been so eager to give her the job.

"Wasn't planning on going home yet." She admitted.

Frank's announcement caught Reggie's attention and suddenly the air was filled with the enraged yells of Reggie, from deep inside the store, but Frank continued without care.

She grabbed his arm and caught his attention. "I need to buy some stuff. Household items, you know, for my apartment. So..."

Frank's mouth stretched into a broad grin over his gleaming white teeth. He clapped his hands together and rubbed his palms in anticipation. "Then I'll drop you off somewhere good. Have you been across the bridge yet? Nicer stores over there if you can afford it." Frank placed a hand on her shoulder and ushered her back across the room. The shrill tone of the door sounded as he pushed open the door and yanked Alex out of the coffee shop, letting the door shut behind them.

"Uhm..." Alex hummed, as Reggie continued to curse Frank's name. He appeared on the other side of the glass, his face filled with rage. "Are you sure about this?" She asked hesitantly, gesturing to Reggie screaming at him from the other side of the window.

"Course! No better tour guide around. I'll show you the ins and outs of Kenzo. Besides, it's not like I have anything else better to do."

The glass door framed Reggie's round face as he started to bang against the glass. He alternated between shaking his fist in Frank's direction and hitting against the glass, but the object of his frustration barely flinched.

"Come on, then." Frank wrapped his arm around Alex as Reggie continued to yell at his back. The sounds were becoming less frequent as if Reggie was running out of steam.

As they walked away from the building, a luxurious car whipped into the parking lot of *The Hideaway*. The car door opened and out walked a tall man neatly dressed in a suit. He looked to be around the same age as Henry, and just as friendly. He glared at Frank as they passed him.

"Hey," Frank called out to the man, "You seen Nichols? Charlie was looking for-"

"Not now." The man snapped as he barrelled past them. Frank saluted his back, as the other man stalked into the coffee shop.

Frank chuckled. "That's," He jerked his head towards the man, "Victor Caine. Used to be friends with him, before he started working for some rich bitch in Belamour. Now, he's too good for us." Frank shrugged. "Aw, well. Never was a ray of sunshine, anyway."

He slapped Alex on the back and led the two of them around *The Hideaway* to the back of the coffee shop, where his truck stood waiting.

It looked a lot like Henry's truck, but this one was clearly much older, though it had been maintained much more carefully.

Frank walked her to the passenger side and unlocked the door. After one more glance at *The Hideaway*, Alex slid off her backpack and climbed in while he rounded the truck to the driver's side. At the very least, if she went missing, Reggie would know who was responsible.

Frank dropped into the driver's seat, started the engine and drove them off towards the centre of town.

Just as they pulled away from the coffee shop, in the rearview mirror Alex saw a small, dishevelled white-haired woman appear from around the back of the coffee shop, tottering towards Victor. He scowled in disgust and stormed inside *The Hideaway*.

CHAPTER 10

Frank had decided to drop her off in Carina for her to shop. The stores were better there than in Rossum or Brewster, but not as expensive as stores in Duval, Luery or Wilmar. He had even been kind enough to point out the bus stops that would take her back to Troye.

He had driven her through Brewster, pointing out his favourite bars, while swearing to 'the good Lord above' that he wasn't an alcoholic, he just liked alcohol. She didn't challenge him on it.

Personally, Alex didn't drink. Not for any concrete reason. She liked a clear head. The idea seemed to confuse Frank.

"So, you don't drink?" He asked as they drove through the busy streets.

"No."

He glanced at her, puzzled. "And you don't read newspapers. Or watch TV. Or talk to people."

Alex pursed her lips, but she stayed silent.

Ahead of them, the traffic light turned red and they came to a stop. "So what did you do? You know, back home?"

"Not much."

"Huh. Any friends?"

"I had a few."

Frank chuckled as the light changed to orange and then green. "If you don't want to tell me, that's fine. No worries."

Alex leaned back in her seat, pressing her head against the headrest. "I thought your brother was the cop, not you."

Frank scoffed. "Not a cop. Not in the slightest." He glanced at her again. "You have something against cops."

Alex shook her head. "No. I just don't know why you want to know so much about me."

"We're co-workers." He drawled. "I'm just making conversation. You keep dodging it."

"Well, I'm sorry. I'm just not that interesting." Her eyes drifted to the dashboard and saw a small toy frog with a hat sitting on it. "Are you close with your brother?"

"Sure. He's my brother. 'Course I love him. My mom would have beat my ass if I didn't. Then my dad. In fact, there probably would've been a long line of relatives ready to whoop my ass."

This time Alex did smile, but it melted away when she thought of Henry and Marcia's comments about him and his daughter. "Did he tell you about what Marcia Rosen said a few nights ago?"

Frank raised an eyebrow. "Are you talking about that annoying lady leaving leaflets everywhere? There was something about her in the paper. She died, didn't she?"

Alex picked at her fingernails. "Yeah," she whispered. "That's the one."

Frank glanced over again at Alex as she shrank in on herself, pulling at her chipped nails. "What did she say?" He pushed.

"She mentioned his daughter." She sighed, as her mind ran through every altercation with the woman. Alex hadn't known her long, but Marcia sure had left an impression on her.

"Juno?" Frank's expression darkened as he turned the wheel of his truck. He parked the car along a road, in front of a block of stores. "What did she say?" He whispered as he turned off the engine. His words had been so soft, that Alex almost didn't catch them.

"She thought that Henry wasn't trying to help her with her daughter Marie when he'd want people to help him if his daughter went missing. How old is she anyway?"

"Thirteen." He growled.

Alex didn't know what to say to that. She had known that Marcia had been wrong to drag Detective Lovett's daughter into this but to know that Marcia was comparing her adult daughter with Henry's thirteen-year-old daughter, came as a shock. Surely, she knew how old Juno was, if she knew he had a daughter.

Next to her, Frank seemed to be thinking the same thing. He dragged a hand over his face before he turned back to look at her. He seemed to have aged in the last few seconds.

"My brother's a good man. A good cop. A good father. A shitty brother, but..." He shrugged. "Can't win 'em all. But he does try. Wish everybody else would see that, especially before they started writing articles. Anyway." He pointed to the building they were in front of. "Here we are."

Alex grabbed the straps of her bag and opened the door. She climbed out and stepped onto the pavement. "I'll see you at work."

Frank gave her a lazy salute. "I'll see you then." He started the engine and joined the trail of cars leading away from the building she was standing in front of.

Now that she had a clearer view, she could see that it was a small household store. As he had warned, everything in there looked expensive.

As she prepared to step into a store that would hand out a receipt that would make her cry, out of the corner of her eye she saw a dark-haired woman putting up flyers on the brick wall of the building. Every once in a while, the woman's eyes would flick over to her and dart back in fear of being caught.

Alex had no idea why she would have taken an interest in her, but she had decided to ignore her. She was sick of flyers. For some reason, everyone seemed to have them. The last two women that had accosted her with their flyers had quickly become two people, whose company Alex didn't enjoy.

As she attempted to walk into the store, however, the woman dropped her flyers on the ground in front of Alex before she could.

Alex crouched to pick up the flyers, and it was then that the woman acknowledged her. She gave her a small, bashful smile when she saw her. "Thanks."

Alex gathered the flyers on the ground in front of her and handed them to her, standing up to her full height and preparing to walk away.

"Wait!" The woman called, as she stood up. "Can I ask you something?"

Alex hesitated. "What?"

"I'm sorry, I just saw you- that man in the truck? The one that dropped you off? Was that Frank Lovett?"

"Yeah, he's my new work colleague." Alex looked down curiously at the woman. She wore a brown jacket, jeans, a green sweater and white sneakers. Her tan handbag was slung over her shoulder. She didn't seem like the type to interact with someone like Frank. He was rough and laid-back. This woman...well, Alex didn't know her, but she handed out flyers, and if the past few days were anything to go by, then Alex already knew what sort of person she was. "Is he a friend of yours?"

The woman made a face. "He's an old friend of my husband's" She corrected.

"Really?"

The woman nodded. "I'm Irene Caine. My husband's Victor Caine."

Alex's eyes widened at the information. The small woman in front of her was very different from the lumbering man she had seen at *The Hideaway*.

"Here." Irene handed her a flyer. It was a simple but tasteful flyer for an event in Belamour. "Have you heard about this?" She gestured to the flyers.

"Uh, no, no. I haven't" And there was nothing that was going to make her go to this one. She had already been roped into too many events.

Irene inhaled shakily and gave Alex a sad smile. Her hands neatly sorted through the flyers and she sniffled. "I'm sorry, it's just...I don't know...a friend of mine died recently and, erm..." she sniffled again. "This event was just gonna be a fundraiser, you know, where we talked about some issues in the community. This was all her. She was the one running the show, and now..." Irene pressed a hand to her mouth and sobbed. It caught in her throat as she tried and failed to push it down.

Uncertainly, Alex took a step forward and patted her gently on her arm. "I'm sorry." She wasn't sure what else to say, but it seemed to soothe the Irene.

"Thanks. She was a bitch. But she was my friend, probably one of the only real ones. People can be too fake around here." She wiped her eyes. "I'm sorry, I'm sorry. You don't know me."

"No, no." Alex insisted. "It's fine."

"It's just such a shame, especially the way she died...I mean...Like I said, Marcie was a bitch, but the right kind of bitch. The no-nonsense type. You knew where you stood with her. I prefer that than...I'm sorry, you don't even know her."

Alex didn't need to ask who she was talking about. Even in death, Marcia Rosen seemed determined to haunt her. That kind of persistence was admirable.

Alex continued to pat Irene's arm slowly. Recently it felt like all she did was ask blunt, invasive questions, but still, she had to ask. "You're talking about Marcia Rosen right?"

Irene nodded. "Yeah, you heard about her?"

"We ran into each other once. What happened?"

Irene smiled sadly. "She was found in her home, with a blow to the back of the head." She sniffed, dragging the back of her hand under her nose. She looked up at Alex. "No one knows what happened. Probably started a fight with the wrong person, huh?"

Tears ran from her eyes as they darted around desperately as if looking around for something to stem the flow of emotions. "I know that's the first thing people say- that she deserved it because she was just an overbearing bitch, who ran her daughter away, but that's not true. She and Marie were close. Marie was always patient and kind, and sure Marcia fussed too much, but whenever she came over to babysit our kids, she was always talking about the trips they went on, the ice skating. A real momma's girl. Made me jealous that my daughter didn't spend that much time with me."

Irene looked up at Alex, and tears streamed from her eyes. "I've known the Rosens since Marie was seven. She wanted to travel, but that girl would never just pack up and leave. She wouldn't have left without saying goodbye." Irene's voice broke on the last word and she started to cry. Her breathing was uneven as she tried to inhale through her tears. Her face became red and she started coughing in between wet gasps. "I'm sorry for...being a mess."

Alex swallowed thickly and shook her head. "It's fine. What have Marie's friends said?"

Irene rolled her eyes. "Nina- Uhm, that's Marie's best friend- says that she went off. Apparently, she was talking about leaving for a while..." Irene wiped at her face. "...but she won't say much more. It's not a good time for her. She's been upset since her therapist, Elise, died. I guess I can't blame her for that. You've probably heard of her too. It was in the news a few weeks ago."

Elise...

Elise...

...Chambers.

Elise Chambers. Apartment 14.

That was the only Elise Alex knew of. The previous owner of her apartment. The name had been at the back of her mind every time she left her apartment. It was almost as if they saw her as some kind of vulture, preying on a tragedy for her gain. She had seen this with Greg and Spencer.

Alex cleared her throat. "Yeah, I did. she lived in my apartment."

Irene's eyes widened in surprise. "You live in Troye then?"

Irritated, Alex folded her arms over her chest. Her dreams of laying low were slipping away.

No...speeding away felt like a more accurate description. She hadn't made it a week and almost everyone knew her name.

"An animal attacked her while she was hiking, right? The neighbours seem pretty shaken up by it."

Irene sniffled. "I doubt anyone there knew her well." She muttered.

"Sorry?"

Irene wiped her eyes. "Elise hadn't lived there long. She used to live in Belamour, with her husband, but there were financial issues, namely his gambling. She left him but didn't have a penny to her name, so Nicki, erm Nicolette got her a deal in *Cassandra's Palace*, with Vincent Sullivan, I think his name is." Irene looked thoughtful for a second before her eyes flicked up to meet Alex's.

"I never understood why she put her there, to be honest. The place is a sty." Irene's eyes snapped to Alex. "Sorry."

Alex thought back to the large, looming building, with all of its cracks and the list of faults everyone at the residents' meeting had given. "No, you're right, it's a dump."

"It's just that Nicolette can afford a much better place than that, especially for her own daughter's therapist. Not sure if that's an ethical issue. Anyway, I'm sure she could have given her a discounted price at one of her own apartment complexes. She's got a bunch. But I guess it kept her away from all of the wagging tongues. The best thing after all of that would be some privacy."

"I agree."

Alex's attention peaked at the words 'daughter's therapist' and the mention of a Nicolette. That wasn't a common name, and it wasn't common enough that Marcia could know two of them. But still, it was best to make sure. "So, this Nicolette?" She prodded.

"Nina's mom. She's a friend of mine and Marcia's. Well, she was more Marcia's friend than mine. Runs a very successful real-estate business. Whenever you're ready to move out of that pit, she's the one you call." She sighed as she wiped the last of her tears. "She's taken over organising the event. In honour of Marcia."

Along with the shadow of Elise, the memories of her encounter with both Marcia and Nicolette felt like a cloud that followed her wherever she went. As if that was the reason for Marcia's death. She knew it wasn't but the guilt hung over her just the same.

She reached out a hand towards the flyers. "Let me have half. The two of us will finish it quicker."

Irene beamed and handed half of the leaflets to her. "Thank you. You don't have to."

Alex returned her smile. "I know, I just want to help. I kinda feel bad for taking up so much of your time." She looked down at the flyers in her hands.

"I should be saying that to you. Anyway, are you thinking about going?"

Alex shook her head. "I live all the way in Troye and I don't think I have the clothes for this."

Irene smirked. "Neither do I. I guess that's why they look at me funny. Hey, why don't we finish up, meet back here and I'll get you a coffee to say thank you."

"Sure."

They divided the street, with their stack of leaflets, and passed them out to each of the stores. It didn't take longer than half an hour before they were both sat at a coffee table inside one of the nicest coffee shops Alex had ever set foot in.

Irene had taken Alex to Belamour and despite the faux casual atmosphere, Alex felt underdressed. She sat delicately, sipping carefully at the rich coffee while Irene rattled on about her week.

"I just think she should be more sensitive, about the subject. But sensitivity," Irene stated, as she sprinkled sugar into her coffee. "Sensitivity isn't her strong suit."

Alex sipped slowly as she tried to understand why Irene's friend lacked tact when asking her daughter about her friends. Alex's eyes had drifted from Irene to the glass door of the cafe as it swung open and Rachel walked in. Quickly, Alex pulled her eyes back to Irene, who hadn't appeared to notice anything, until Rachel walked over to join them.

Irene looked up as Rachel arrived at their table and smiled brightly at her. She pulled out a seat. "Thank you for joining us.

Rachel glanced at Alex before looking back at Irene, thank you for having me. "Hello again," She added to Alex.

Alex stretched her mouth into a smile. "Hi." A heavy pit sank in Alex's stomach as Rachel took a seat next to her.

"I'm sorry, this is Alex," Irene began. She turned back to Alex apologetically, "I was supposed to meet her here, I hope you don't mind if she joins us."

Alex chuckled awkwardly, unsure what she could say apart from *of course not*. Anything else would just be rude. "Of course not." She smiled at Rachel, as the woman watched her warily.

Rachel turned to Alex. "I suppose you've heard about Marcia Rosen by now." Rachel began.

Alex nodded. "Yeah, I did. Detective Lovett and Detective Li told me when they came by the bookstore."

Rachel looked surprised. "Did they? They didn't mention anything to me."

Irene cleared her throat. "Speaking of which, I was thinking about Detectives Lovett and Li and their mishandling of all of the missing people, the animal attacks. I think Marcia's murder should put pressure on them to fix things. Right? I mean, she was the one shouting the loudest and look at what happened. And if they don't listen, get them fired."

It took a few seconds of disbelief for Alex to register that she was witnessing a plot against David and Henry. It really shouldn't have surprised her if Irene was close friends with Marcia.

Rachel's eyes widened. "Erm, perhaps that's a bit much to ask for."

Irene frowned. "Isn't that what you wanted? To put a spotlight on their negligence."

Rachel chuckled nervously. "I wanted to look into the missing people, and the lack of attention they are given, I don't want to punish the detectives."

Irene's expression turned icy. "That's the same thing, isn't it? They failed at their job and now we want people to know."

Alex had to admit that there, Irene had a point. Rachel's article would, inadvertently or not, put more pressure on the leading detectives. Blame would be placed on them regardless of culpability. No one would care if they were guilty or not. Some people already thought they were responsible and this article would only give more credibility to their suspicions. Wasn't that always Rachel's goal? Why stop now?

Irene pulled back and her eyes flickered to Alex for support. Alex couldn't give it. Just as she opened her mouth to give a hopefully better refusal than Rachel had, the door to the coffee shop opened again and in walked a familiar chestnut-haired woman in another spectacular suit. A sullen girl whom Alex had only ever seen once in a photograph with Marie Rosen, shuffled behind her, wearing a baggy t-shirt and jeans.

Nicolette James raised a hand and waved in their direction. Irene waved back. It only took a few seconds for her eyes to land on Alex hunched over in her chair.

"Nicolette." Irene greeted. She craned her head around Nicolette to look at the girl behind her. "Hey, Nina."

The girl named Nina pulled back so that she was blocked completely from Irene's view. "Hi." She mumbled.

Nicolette looked back and with a gentle hand, ushered the girl away to the counter. "Sweetie, why don't you go get us our drinks, ok?" Nina obeyed and slouched off to the counter.

Nicolette turned back and shook her head apologetically. "Sorry about her."

Rachel shook her head. "It's okay. We understand. How are her therapy sessions going?"

"Not well, she doesn't want to see anyone else."

"Poor thing," Irene added. She turned to Alex. "This is Alex, she was helping me pass out the flyers."

"Oh, yes, I remember you. Our last meeting was...unpleasant, but I still hope that we can put it behind us."

"Me too." Alex agreed.

Nicolette's eyes roamed from Irene, back to Alex, to Rachel. "So how's the article going?"

"It's not."

Nicolette raised a brow. "Really?" She brushed her hair back from her face and took a seat next to Irene with an exaggerated sigh. "You know after Elise died, Nina really shut herself down. I don't think she wants to open up to anyone else. Things are too raw for her. First, her best friend runs off, and then when things are getting settled with her therapist, she dies. How much can one girl go through?"

Irene nodded sympathetically. "Do you want me to talk to her?"

Nicolette shook her head but patted Irene's arm. "Thanks, but I think it's best to just give her some time." Nicolette looked up as Nina joined them. She placed the cup in front of Nicolette as she hovered behind her, holding her takeaway cup in her hands. Her eyes stayed trained on the floor in front of her.

Irene craned her head to meet Nina's eyes, but she didn't seem to notice.

Nicolette tapped Nina on her arm. "Nina, you remember Rachel Ellis, don't you? She's the reporter, who's writing an article about missing people."

Nina nodded, as her eyes roamed around the shop. She was the only person standing but made no move to sit. When her eyes landed on Alex, they narrowed. "Who's she?"

"Alex," Alex answered crisply. "Just moved to Troye."

Nina's throat worked. Irene looked between Alex and Nina. "She's living in Elise's old apartment."

Nicolette's eyes snapped to Alex. "Really? So soon?"

Annoyed, she repeated the same thing she had since she had gotten to Kenzo. "I didn't know anything when I paid for it. I only found out when one of my neighbours told me." She was getting tired of having to justify it.

"That's pretty scummy of Vincent! He should have said something."

"I'm not mad. It was pretty cheap, so I was expecting a lot worse." Alex sipped the last of her coffee and stood. "Sorry, but I've got to go." She glanced out the window at the darkening sky. "I was supposed to do some shopping."

"Oh, ok. See you." Irene called.

Rachel and Nicolette added their goodbyes. Nina shoved her hands and followed Alex away from the table. "Yeah, I'm gonna meet some friends."

"When are you gonna be back?" Nicolette called. "Your father called from work. He let us know that he'll be late. But, he wants you to call him after six-"

"Fine. Later! God!" Nina hissed. She stormed around Alex and out of the coffee shop.

Before anyone tried to stop her, Alex slipped out as the door swung back and saw Nina staring blankly at her. She shoved her hand into her pocket and pulled out a pack of cigarettes and a lighter. She took one out, put it in her mouth and lit the end.

She took a long drag and exhaled slowly. "You met my mom?"

Alex rubbed at her eyes. "Yeah, and Marcia."

"Where?"

"In a supermarket."

Nina chuckled darkly. "Oh, I think they mentioned you. The street-urchin of Troye. Congratulations, you were worth breaking open the strong stuff. Went through a bottle and a half talking about you."

Alex rolled her eyes. "I'm glad." She deadpanned. She walked around Nina, but the girl fell into step next to her.

The choice surprised Alex, but considering what Nina had lost, she could understand it.

"I'm sorry about your therapist. And your friend."

Nina sniffed. "Me too."

Nina walked alongside her until they reached the bus stop. She had even boarded the same bus as her, saying that she just wanted to sit. She hadn't said much, apart from a few less-than-pleasant comments about Marcia.

Alex hadn't wanted to mention Marie anymore than she already had, but that seemed to be the elephant sitting between them.

"How long have you known Marie?" Alex asked softly.

"Since we were seven." Nina sniffed. "I ran away from my mom and dad and bumped into her. Convinced her to follow me to the park. You know, Belamour's park, with the massive oak tree?" She pouted at the memory. "How was I supposed to know she couldn't climb a tree for shit?" She chewed at her fingernails. "Marcia didn't stop bitching all the way to the hospital. Hasn't stopped bitching about it since. Even Marie's dad, Richard, didn't get so mad.

Marie didn't. You'd think the person who actually broke their arm would be mad, but..."

A very vivid picture of Marcia marching a younger version of herself, crying, with a broken arm, flooded Alex's mind. "She thought that Marie didn't run away."

Nina turned her wide brown eyes on Alex. Her brows had furrowed. "She's made that clear." She sniffed again as her eyes filled with tears. "Can I tell you something? Swear you won't, you know, go back and tell my mom, or anything, right?"

The nod that Alex gave was out of reflex more than anything else, but now that she had made the promise, she had no desire to break it. "Tell me."

Tears began to run from the corner of Nina's eyes. "I miss her."

"Marie?"

Nina shook her head as she wiped her eyes. "Yeah, but I wasn't talking about her. I meant...Marcia." Her tears ran more freely now. "I know it's only been...what, a day, but... it's like...it's like..."

"She reminded you of Marie?" Alex finished.

Nina nodded helplessly and started to cry harder. "I didn't even like her...but, she..." she rubbed her eyes and looked around self-consciously.

"I understand." While Alex had seen and experienced loss, she never knew what to say, or do about it. The words she was supposed to say always sounded hollow when she heard them leave her mouth. But she knew that Nina didn't need any words, she just wanted someone to talk to. A stranger who wouldn't judge her, who would probably forget their conversation as soon as they parted.

"Do you know where Marie is? Have you told her about her mom?"

Nina tensed in her seat. She shook her head. "No."

Alex didn't know if she was saying 'no' to her first question, or her second, but she thought it best not to push her anymore.

As their bus approached another stop, Nina stood from her seat abruptly. "I'll see you." She called over her shoulder and slipped off the bus.

As Alex looked out of the window, at the darkening sky above, she wondered if she had asked too much. Had she asked too many questions? Did Nina think that she had only spoken to her out of curiosity? Had she made the mistake of leaving Nina alone?

She knew Nina wasn't her responsibility, and she was an adult, but she was also upset and while Alex didn't like meddling in other people's affairs, even when invited to, her mind kept going back to Nina.

It was only after she had stepped off the bus did she remember why she had been in Belamour in the first place. With a sigh, she began the walk home.

Perhaps, she should just forget about furnishing her apartment. The way things were going, she would have to leave soon anyway.

Perhaps, her dream of a home was too much to ask.

CHAPTER 11

When Alex arrived back at *The Palace*, the interior was even darker than it was when she left a few hours ago. One of the issues that had been raised at the meeting had been that the lightbulbs that lined the hallways were always blown. Many residents had various issues of their own that they wanted to raise, but this was one of the few that everyone wholeheartedly agreed on, and now that Alex had been submerged in darkness, she did too.

The door to *Cassandra's Palace* opened with a loud ominous creak that echoed around the room. She could see why people were scared about security when the place looks like an abandoned building most of the time and it was. No one had seen Sully in ages. She stepped into the foyer and out of the corner of her eye, she saw shadows.

The main door slammed closed behind her and shut out the outside noise. The silence muffled her ears, and the loss of it put her on edge. Her eyes darted around, fighting against the darkness. Her ears strained for the sounds of the other residents.

She had left before the rest of them the night of the meeting and hoped that once out of sight, they would lose interest and forget about her. She hadn't seen them since.

After all, it was just a bad coincidence that she had run into the creature in the first place. Despite what they likely suspected, she didn't know much more than they did. She just wanted to get to her apartment, lock the door behind her and hope that the mess of the last few days would fade away.

The soft patter of her feet as she scurried through the main entrance was the only sound to be heard but when it was joined by a soft gasp, it stopped abruptly.

She spun around, searching for the sound. Her eyes moved over the shapes in the dark, until they settled on the silhouette of a small boy in front of her.

His hair was black, almost blending in with the shadows around him, and the contrast between his pale skin and his hair made him look even paler. He was almost swallowed by the long brown coat he wore and the black backpack on his bag pulled his shoulders down. His knobbly fingers picked at the straps of his bags as he stared up at her, uncertain.

Alex wasn't sure how old he was, but she was pretty sure he couldn't be above thirteen and she wouldn't guess under ten. His cheeks were still chubby from childhood. His eyes darted around the room and he looked ready to run at a moment's notice.

"Hi." She offered.

"Hi." The boy mumbled.

Alex looked around into the dark, searching for anyone else. When she found no one, her eyes returned to him. He stared at her with wide watchful eyes. Like clockwork, they darted around the room before returning to Alex, and back again.

"Do you live here?" Alex asked.

The boy flinched and frowned down at his feet, but nodded his head. "Do you?" He asked in return.

"Yeah, I just moved in. It's been a few days. I think. I haven't been keeping track of time."

The boy eyed her with some suspicion. "Did you go to the meeting?"

"Yeah, I did. You weren't there were you?"

The boy shook his head. "No, but my mom went."

"Oh. I didn't get much time to meet anyone personally, but I'm sure she'll recognize me." She muttered under her breath. Understanding dawned on the boy's face.

"I think she did mention you."

Alex gritted her teeth. "Great."

She took a few steps towards the stairwell. "Anyway, I guess I'll see you around, kid. Night-"

"Wait!" The boy cried out. As soon as he did, he clamped his mouth shut and looked around again.

"Yeah?" Alex prompted him. "What's wrong?"

The boy hesitated for a moment before he took a step forward. "Can you...uhm? I was gonna go to the shop, but my mom says...that I shouldn't go on my own, but she's not here and I wanted to get something to eat from the shop." The boy looked up at her hopelessly, and Alex sighed.

"Don't you have anything at home? Where's your mom?"

"She's at work and...I ate my sandwich at school." He trailed off.

She wasn't a babysitter, nor did she have the desire to become one, but if she left the boy alone and something happened to him after she left, wouldn't that make her responsible? Her neighbours might think so.

That would bump her up on the list of suspects with the residents and the police.

And she wouldn't blame them for it.

But even if that weren't the case, she still wasn't sure that she could just leave the boy alone in the dark. Not while he was still staring at her like a stray pup.

"You want me to go with you to the shop?"

Hesitantly, the boy nodded.

She sighed. "Sure. Fine." She relented. "Let's go."

"Thanks!" The boy ran to her side as she walked back to the front door. He kept his distance but made sure to stay with her, every step she took.

She pulled open the main door, and he ducked under her arm eagerly.

Once they were outside the boy took the lead and steered them to the left, back down the path she had just travelled.

"So what's your name?" She asked.

"Cecil."

"And where do you live?'

"On the fifth floor with my mom Lydia Dawson. She's a nurse at Kenzo General Hospital. Where do you live?"

"On the second floor."

The boy glanced up at her. "Do you mean apartment 14? Where that lady who died, lived?"

"Yup," Alex answered blandly.

"Yeah. My mom did mention you after the meeting. She said that the police had talked to you, but she didn't know what."

"Yeah, well..."

"Was it about the lady in your apartment?"

"No. How about we just forget about all of that and get you something to eat." Alex snapped.

The boy clamped his lips together and remained silent until they reached the entrance of a shop. It was lit up with neon lights in the window display.

The boy charged ahead up an aisle, picked a sandwich off the shelf, and a drink from the fridge and zoomed back to the cashier in under 30 seconds. He picked up a chocolate bar from the rack in front of them and placed them alongside his sandwich.

He took his money from his pocket and placed it on the counter next to his items. The man at the till gave him his change, and Cecil rushed back out onto the street.

The boy had already eaten half of his sandwich before they had gotten twelve feet away. He had juggled his items in his arms to hold his drink, and his chocolate bar and eat his sandwich as he walked.

Alex reached out and took the drink and chocolate bar from under his arm while he continued to wolf down his sandwich.

"When was the last time you ate?"

Cecil blushed. The red that tinted his cheeks was visible even at night. "I ate at school. My mom took an extra shift and there was nothing left to eat at home. She was supposed to go shopping when she got home."

"Why were you waiting at the entrance in the dark?"

Cecil was silent as he chewed. "I was waiting there."

"What's wrong with your apartment?"

"Nothing," he answered sullenly.

"Don't you have any games to play?"

"Sure," he muttered.

"But you'd rather sit in the dark?"

"I just-" he stopped abruptly with a huff.

His mouth pressed itself into a tight line and he looked unwilling to say more.

"Were you scared?"

Cecil blushed again but didn't answer.

"You know," Alex offered lightly, "everyone at the meeting was getting pretty scared about the animal lurking around. I wouldn't blame you for getting scared too."

He looked up at her with narrowed eyes. His nose had scrunched as he thought over her words. They had reached the main doors of *Cassandra's Palace*. He looked at the building in front of him, and his anxiety seemed to increase. He shifted on his feet, pulling away from Alex.

She looked up at the building. "Is it because your mom's not at home?"

Hesitantly, he nodded.

"Well, then you can stay with me 'til she comes back."

He looked up at her and his face lit up. "Really?"

"Sure. I even have frozen pizza if you get hungry again."

He opened his mouth to say something but changed his mind at the last second. "Are you sure?" He said finally.

"I'm sure. Rather than you skulking around here alone. Whatever that animal is, it's not safe for you to be outside on your own. Especially at night." She smiled at him, and she could feel the muscles around her mouth creak from lack of use. Cecil smiled back, and they both entered *Cassandra's*.

As they entered, Alex immediately noticed the difference. At the end of the hallway, the door to Sully's office was ajar, and the man himself was moving around his office.

After everything Alex had heard about him today, she was surprised to see him. She walked to the end of the hall and tapped on his door. The soft swear he uttered was enough to tell her he hadn't expected to be caught.

She pushed open the door and in front of her stood the elusive landlord.

The tension in his body was visible as he glared at her. "Yes?" he answered tersely.

"Angela's looking for you. Everyone is. There was a meeting a few nights ago. You missed it."

"Oh, did I?" he asked acidly.

"Yup. No one can find you when they need you. I wonder why."

The man glared at her from across his desk. "Is there anything you need? I'm quite busy right now."

"Not me, no. But Angela has a list of stuff that needs doing. Some of it includes security issues."

Sully's jaw clenched even tighter and Alex swore she could hear his teeth grinding together.

"It's a nice building though," she continued. "Even with all the problems. I imagine it must be difficult trying to pacify the local busybodies."

Sully scoffed. "That's an understatement. Some of them exist to complain. And when one of them starts, the others jump on the bandwagon."

"Well, we won't keep you. Just thought you should know before you disappear again."

With that, both Alex and Cecil left Sully's office and went up the stairs to Alex's apartment.

She took a frozen pizza from the freezer, unwrapped it and after turning on the oven, threw it in.

Cecil had eaten half of his pizza by the time she sat down to eat hers. The pizza must have loosened his tongue because he started to talk.

"I think I saw the monster that is killing all those people."

Alex chewed her pizza slowly. "Really?" she mumbled.

Cecil nodded earnestly. "The lady that lived here, ran into it the night she died. She followed it somewhere."

"How do you know this?"

The boy hesitated as if questioning his certainty. "I saw them through the window."

Alex put her pizza down on her plate. "What did you see?"

The boy chewed his lip again. "The old lady on the ground floor. I think she ate the lady from this apartment."

It wasn't the strangest thing Alex had ever heard, but it was certainly a different take from what most thought was terrorising Kenzo. She hadn't been aware of an old lady in the complex. She thought she had seen just about everyone at the meeting and she couldn't recall anyone being mentioned as absent.

Cecil seemed quite guarded, so if he was telling this story to Alex, he believed it.

"Did you...see it happen?"

Cecil shook his head. "No, but she went off with the old lady and went missing."

"Why do you think this old lady has anything to do with it?"

Cecil looked around the apartment and spoke in a lower voice. "I see her out on the street at night when no one else is around. She's just walking around outside at night."

"Have you seen her anywhere else?"

Cecil nodded. "I see her everywhere. I saw her in the park, at the mall with my mom. Sometimes on my way to school."

"Are you sure it's the same person?"

Cecil nodded again, more earnestly this time. "It's her. She's got this blue coat she always wears. All the time."

"Have you seen her do anything?"

The space between his eyebrows became pinched. "No." he pouted. "She's really scary. Sometimes I think she's watching me."

Alex nodded. "Okay." She said evenly.

Cecil deflated in his seat. "You don't believe me, do you? My mom doesn't."

"I believe you saw something. I just want to understand what that is."

Cecil was silent for a few moments before he added his final piece of evidence. "She has yellow eyes at night."

Alex turned to watch the small boy sitting in front of her. He stared up at her with a focus and determination that concerned her.

He wasn't lying, but that didn't mean he was right, either. His imagination was probably working overtime with his mother at work. He had nothing but time to come up with all kinds of scenarios.

"Let's have some ice cream, okay?" She offered.

Cecil's shoulder slouched. "Sure."

"But, I do believe you, you know."

Cecil looked up apprehensively. "You do?"

Alex nodded. "I'm pretty sure that I saw...something...something that other people might not believe."

Cecil opened his mouth as if to say something when they heard the sound of footsteps passing across the floor.

"I think that's Spencer," Cecil said, standing and walking to the door. "He lives on this floor."

"Oh, *him*," Alex muttered.

Alex stood, as Cecil pressed his ear against the door to listen. He waited for a moment before he unlocked the door and twisted the handle. The door swung open and they saw Spencer standing in front of his door, holding his keys in his hand. He turned around to look at them

His eyes moved between both Cecil and Alex. "Cecil, what are you doing here? Where's Lydia?"

"She's at work."

Spencer's eyes flitted over Alex for a second, before he gestured to Cecil. "Why don't you come with me, Cecil? I'll take you upstairs. Get your stuff."

Cecil looked at Alex for confirmation and she nodded. Hesitantly, he grabbed his bag and his coat and walked over to Spencer as they walked up the stairs.

As Alex stood alone in her apartment, she tried not to feel upset about how Spencer had reacted, but it was just another reminder that not only was she not blending in, she wasn't making friends either.

CHAPTER 12

The next few days flew past in a misty haze. Alex would wake up in the early hours of the morning, struggling against the smothering shadows and chill that had filled her apartment in the night.

On her days off, she would lay around all day.

But on the days she had to work, she'd eat a slice of toast, shower for five minutes and dress in her uniform before the sleep had even left her eyes, before rushing out of her apartment.

The hallways were always devoid of light and life, leaving Alex alone with her thoughts that always felt too loud in the silence. It was only when she walked past the first floor, that a chill would walk down her spine and her thoughts would quieten.

Without any lights in the hallway, she felt uneasy, tensing at any creak she heard or flicker of movement she saw. Every time she walked past the landing, she felt watched, though there was no one around. She had made an effort to keep a lower profile whenever she was inside of the building but out of her apartment, since the resident's meeting and her last encounter with Spencer.

Since she hadn't spoken to any of her neighbours since then, she had no idea what they thought of her if they even thought anything, but she didn't know how to ask them without looking even more suspicious.

The walk to and from *The Hideaway* was always a cold trek, but one that passed in an uneventful blur. When she arrived at *The Hideaway*, she was always welcomed by the warmth of the interior, the bright artificial light and the sleepy gaze of Frank.

"Oh, good. You're here." He yawned. "Let's get this done."

Reggie had left Frank in charge while he ran some errands. Frank was also in charge of Alex and was responsible for her training.

As a teacher, Frank preferred to be hands-off and would only get up from his seat to show Alex how to use the different machines and the way they worked.

As a student, Alex had caught on quickly, only needing to be shown something once before she got the hang of it, something that Frank seemed to appreciate since he didn't have to move from his seat behind the counter.

She didn't mind doing most of the work as it kept her mind from wandering to darker topics. But that was hard when every time she looked up she would see newspaper articles talking about Marcia Rosen's death.

Customers would come in and she would hear whispers about the investigation and speculation about things that had happened. Thankfully though her name didn't seem to pop up anywhere.

She was wiping down a table when the bell above the door chimed and in walked Spencer. Once he caught sight of her behind the counter, his stride stuttered but he continued until he reached in front of her.

"I didn't know you worked here." His smooth voice announced.

Alex shrugged. "Detective Lovett talked to his friend and got me the job."

Spencer frowned. "He did?"

Alex nodded, her fingers fiddling with the rag in her hand. "What would you like?"

"Coffee. Black. One sugar, no milk. To go."

Alex nodded and reached for a takeaway cup. There was silence as she put together his drink, and she could tell Spencer was watching her.

"How do you know Detective Lovett?" She asked as she poured the coffee.

"I'm a coroner. I work with dead bodies so we work together a lot."

"Him and Detective Li?" Alex said. Once she had finished with his order, she put the cover over his cup. "Do you know what happened with Marcia?"

"I can't say anything. I'm sure you know that." Spencer says finally.

"I just mean, did it have anything to do with the animal or is it something separate-"

"I can't tell you that. You saw her though, didn't you?"

Alex smiled bitterly. "I'm sure you know that. She was asking me about her daughter, Marie. That reporter woman, Rachel, thought that I would know something and would be able to help."

"Why would she think that?"

Alex shrugged. "The night I arrived, Detective Lovett and Detective Li picked me up from the side of the road and dropped me off at *Freddie's Grill*. We ran into Marcia and Rachel, and Rachel assumed I must be living rough. She thought I might have seen Marie or something. The next morning Marcia passed me again in the middle of a supermarket and she grabbed me and I shouted at her. Next thing I know she's dead."

Spencer's jaw worked as he struggled with something on his mind. "Everybody's just on edge." He said finally.

"Yeah, I guess."

He handed her the money for the drink and gave her a small nod. As she put the money in the till, Frank wandered over. "Morbid, little son of a bitch, isn't he?"

"Well, he is a coroner." Alex muttered.

Frank chuckled, just as the door opened once more and suddenly the humour on his face disappeared. Victor strolled in, wearing a grey suit. He walked up to the counter and addressed Frank.

"You know where I could find Charlie?" He growled.

Frank's jaw tightened. "What do you want him for?"

"Where is he?" Victor repeated.

Frank shrugged in a show of dismissal, as his eyes bored holes into Victor. "Don't know."

His intensity didn't phase Victor. Instead, he turned and walked away from the counter. "Well, when you do see him, tell him I'm looking for him." He called over his shoulder.

Frank stared after him. Alex wanted to ask what that was about but she didn't want to intrude too soon. Frank would tell her when he was ready so she left it up to him.

The rest of the day continued without too many incidents. As they were locking up, Alex picked up one of the newspapers that had been left on the table and looked at the front page. It detailed investigations into Marcia Rosen's death and also about the animal attacks. Unsurprisingly, the newspaper was *Mercury News*.

Frank walked up beside her and took the newspaper from her hands. "I wouldn't go worrying about things you read in that newspaper. They like to exaggerate things a lot. People leave all the time. Not one of them tells everyone when they pick up and go. That woman's just looking for a story and she doesn't care who she hurts. They just want to blame the police for everything. The animal attack, people going missing, that woman, the murders. They want to make it sound like some big conspiracy. It's just a lucky animal and a bunch of unfortunate coincidences. And a few murders."

"Oh, that's ok, then."

Frank rolled his eyes at her. "Bad shit happens everywhere. It's sad, but it is what it is."

"So, you don't think any of these things are linked?"

"Why would they be? One woman did get eaten by an animal, but the rest of the people who'd supposedly gone missing, probably just upped and left. My brother's got enough to deal with without some nosy, ladder-climbing reporter trying to make a name for herself." He shook his head. "Come on, I'll drop you home."

"Thanks."

They locked up and climbed into Frank's truck. As he drove through Rossum, Frank was quiet.

"What's wrong?" Alex asked finally as they waited at a red light. "Is this because of the man that came by earlier?"

"Victor? He's looking for a friend of mine. Don't know why, though."

"Is that a bad thing?"

"It's not a good thing. Charlie's stupid enough to get wrapped up in his business. That usually ends up with Charlie paying for it."

"Why don't you just call him, then."

Frank rubbed his jaw. "The truth is, I haven't heard from him. For at least a week now. Just hope he hasn't gone and done something stupid." He craned his neck out the window and pointed. "You see that pub there? That's where we usually hang out."

"You want us to go see if he's in there?"

Frank's eyes flickered to her for a minute. "No, I don't want to keep you. It's getting dark."

"It's fine, I'll wait if you want to go check." After a moment's hesitation, Frank turned the car and drove around to the parking lot. He cut the engine. "I'll be back in a minute."

Alex waited.

When Frank came back, he looked agitated. He got in the car and drove again. "He wasn't in there."

"That doesn't mean anything bad."

"No, I just..." he stopped abruptly. "That son of a bitch!" He glared out of the window. "There he is, right there!" He pointed at a lanky dark-haired man ahead of them. Frank sighed in relief. He fished in the pocket of his coat and pulled out his phone. Glaring at the man in front of them, he dialled. The man ahead continued to walk on, unbothered. Frank waited impatiently on the phone before he ended the call with a curse.

"Just talk to him later. He seems fine." Alex offered.

Frank exhaled irritably. He turn the key in the ignition and began driving them to *Cassandra's Palace.*

He parked his truck outside of the building and killed the engine.

"Don't read too much into what you hear in the newspaper." He said suddenly. "You start seeing shadows everywhere."

Alex climbed out of his truck and he drove away.

Alex turned and walked up the stairs to the building. Ahead of her, the door opened and Goldie came out. She came to an abrupt halt as she saw Alex. She hesitated for a moment before walking away without a word.

The day after that was uneventful.

On the third day of work, Alex got up early, at six, showered, dressed and ate before leaving her apartment for work, long before sunrise.

It was cold as she walked along the dark streets.

As Alex approached the unlit building, she was surprised to find that *The Hideaway* was still closed. By the time she had left home, it was already past 7 am. So the fact that she had managed to walk to the coffee shop and still arrived before Frank had was concerning.

The sky was a dull grey even as it lightened. With every minute she stood outside, she could see the tidy streets that surrounded the coffee shop and its car park. Far enough for the building to breathe and not be overwhelmed by the spirit of the other buildings, but close enough not to feel isolated.

Alex looked up at the large sign above her head and sighed. She turned and pressed her back against the brick wall beside the glass door. She'd arrived on time. She'd held up her end. Frank had the keys, so she would have to wait for him.

It was pitch dark around her. The air still had the chill from the night before. Alex leaned against the brick wall, looking out at the surrounding buildings. She was drawn back to the night before and she was mad that she was again in a similar situation so soon.

She waited for half an hour before Frank's truck rolled up next to her.

Frank slid out of his truck and raised an eyebrow at her. "How long have you been here?"

"Long enough that I can't feel my toes."

Frank looked down at her feet. "You might need better shoes."

Alex scowled at him and he grinned toothily at her. "Come on." He waved her over. "We've got some work to do. Frank shoved his hand into his pocket and pulled out a ring of silver keys thumbing through them until he found the one he wanted. He picked that key out and slotted it into the lock of *The Hideaway's* main door. He pushed open the doors and sauntered inside the building. Alex peeled her back off the brick wall and followed him inside.

As Frank walked through the coffee shop lazily turning everything on. He turned back to her. "You know, that prick Victor nearly ran me off the fuckin' road? Almost died. Prick."

"Are you okay?"

Frank waved her off but was happy that she was concerned. "Yeah, yeah. Better than he's gonna be, that's for sure. Anyway..."

He waved her over to join him behind the counter. Alex did, taking off her coat as she did.

He grabbed an apple pie from the display, and a large coffee and collapsed at the table nearest the counter. "Didn't eat breakfast," he said around a mouthful of dessert. "You want?"

"No, thanks."

Over the next few hours, more customers dropped by and Alex patiently took their orders while Frank sat in the corner, flipping through another newspaper.

Though she tried to push the chatter of the customers down to an indecipherable drone there were several instances where the conversation between two patrons was clear as a bell. She had been noting down an order, when the bell over the door announced another arrival.

Alex looked up and saw David and Henry enter the coffee shop. Frank sighed in exaggerated disappointment as he closed his newspaper. He made a show of folding it over neatly as the two men approached the counter.

"Coffee, gentlemen? Pastries, perhaps? Some gossip?" He rose from his seat with the same laziness that had caused him to take root beside the counter in the first place. He bared a toothy grin.

"No donuts?" Henry rumbled.

Frank shrugged. "We get 'em but didn't feel like taking a punch for a joke staler than them."

He nodded to Alex. "You sent her?" He asked conversationally.

Both Henry and David glanced in her direction before Henry answered. "Yeah."

"To check up on me?'

Henry scoffed. "No, you idiot, she needed a job. " He turned to Alex. "How's it going?"

"Fine." Alex chirped.

Henry turned to Frank. "Frank-"

"I swear I didn't do anything. Alex tell 'em."

Alex nodded her head in agreement. "Frank hasn't done anything. At all."

Frank's eyes narrowed. "Wait a minute-"

"Yeah, I did everything Frank taught me to do. On my own. All. On. My. Own."

David scowled at Frank. "How do you still have your job? Why hasn't Reggie fired you yet?"

Frank folded his arms over his chest smugly. "Can't fire me if I keep showing up. He has to pay me."

Alex, Henry and David all exchanged a look. Alex cleared her throat. "I don't think that's how that works."

Frank opened his mouth to argue, but Henry held up his hand. "Uh-uh, shut up and get up. Get your ass behind that counter and help her."

Frank's eyes moved from his brother to Alex. He kicked his chair back, like a sullen child and joined Alex behind the counter. Alex tried to keep the smile off of her lips but from the sour expression on Frank's face, he wasn't convinced.

For the rest of her shift, Frank was forced to work alongside her, smiling at the customers with a dangerously sharp grimace.

But that may have something to do with Henry and David watching them from their table on the other side of the room. With every sip of black coffee, Henry kept his menacing glare on his brother, daring him to act up.

He didn't.

Apparently there was someone who could stop Frank's self-indulgent reign. His bigger, scarier brother.

Someone should tell poor Reggie.

Thanks to Henry, Alex finished her shift fifteen minutes earlier, at a quarter to six.

Due to it being the middle of February, the sky overhead had already darkened, by the time she left the warmth of *The Hideaway.*

As Alex walked through the streets, the hair on the back of her neck stood up. At first, she thought it was the cold.

She looked around, still not slowing her pace. Walking slowly behind her was a man in a torn brown jacket. She couldn't see the man's face but she could sense that he was following her.

After a few streets, it became undeniable that she was being followed.

She picked up her pace with every street she turned down, but the person kept a steady pace.

When she finally reached the dilapidated building of *Cassandra's*, she rushed up the stairs, with her keys in her frozen hands, slamming them against the keypad. The door buzzed as she opened the main doors and she slipped inside.

Her heart kept pounding against her ribcage as she ran across the entrance to the stairwell. She scrambled up the stairs to her floor and hastily unlocked the door to her apartment.

Her hands didn't stop shaking, even when she heard the buzzer of the door let the stranger into the building.

CHAPTER 13

Alex kept her ear pressed against the door, as she stood in her dark apartment. She heard a thudding footstep travel through the hall below her until it disappeared behind a door.

An apartment door.

Had she just overreacted?

She told herself that she had, but even still, it took her ten more minutes before she was prepared to peel her ear away from the door.

That night, it took her longer to fall asleep. She lay on her back, staring at the broken ceiling. Her mind was racing, but her eyes were heavy with sleep. When she finally slipped into oncoming darkness, it was with the image of an old lady in a blue coat with yellow orbs for eyes, burned into her mind.

The next few days were relatively quiet, not much happened apart from Cecil coming to visit after school. He told her as much as he knew about Elise Chambers, the woman who used to live in her apartment, but since he was twelve, it wasn't a lot.

When Wednesday arrived, Cecil walked her to her job on his way to school.

She appreciated his company, but she was sure that it brought him more comfort than it did her. She wasn't sure how much he had told his mom about where he went after school, but she had sent him back home with two ready-made meals once, so she assumed she must have some idea.

As soon as the store came into sight, she sent him on his way. Her shift would end long after his school would, so she expected he would show up at her door later.

Inside the store, Frank was already lounging around behind the counter. His expression brightened as soon as he saw her and he gave her a toothy grin. "I'd almost forgotten what you look like. You're early."

Alex looked down at her watch. It said 7:25. Her shift started at 7:45. "Not by much."

"Well, that's good news for me. Reggie's got some boxes that need unpacking and shelves that need stocking, and he doesn't trust me to do it, so he said, 'Frank, make sure Alex goes through each of the boxes and puts them on the correct shelves. You just stay on the till, and let her handle the rest.' So, clearly, he trusts you more than he trusts me."

"He said that, did he?"

"Yep."

"He said that? Already? In my first month?"

Frank shook his head in mock sympathy. "He's a strange man."

Alex had thought or at least hoped that he was joking. And he had been.

It had just been the two of them for most of the day. This time, he'd taken his job as her mentor much more seriously than Alex had thought he would.

Every task that had come with the job was demonstrated, carefully and repeatedly, with Frank stopping every so often to make sure that she understood. He didn't get frustrated or flustered when she made a mistake, he just showed her the correct way to do it, no matter how many times she asked.

But once he was sure that she was fine, he quickly lost interest in his job again and disappeared through the back of the store. She didn't have time to worry about him when she was stuck behind the till.

KENZO

Even after only working at *The Hideaway* for a few days, Alex already knew how to open up the shop without Frank.

By the time he walked in she was ready to open up the cafe.

"You are here early." He muttered.

"It's not that early. You might just be a bit late."

Frank grunted. He took off his coat and headed for the 'employees only' room.

"Hey," she began conversationally, as she wiped down one of the counters. "How long have these animal attacks been going on?"

Frank looked confused by her question for a second before he answered. "About a year."

"And no one knows what the animal is or where it came from?"

Frank shrugged. "No. They think it might be a bear but, who knows?"

"But that's strange, isn't it? That it just...just arrived somehow?"

Frank shrugged again. "Must have wandered here or something."

"But, then that means wherever it came from, someone must know about it. Are there any articles or anything about local bears online?"

Frank shook his head. "No, that was one thing that's always stumped, Henry. That it just popped out of nowhere one day. A smart animal that no one can find. Spooky, isn't it?"

"But other people have been missing too, haven't they?"

"People pick up and leave all the time for different reasons. Just because there's an animal running around town doesn't mean it's responsible for everything. Bad things happen everywhere."

"No, but could the people that have gone missing be victims that no one has found yet."

Frank tossed his coat over the back of a wooden chair at one of the tables and sank down on it. "I doubt it."

"Why? Why are you so sure?"

"Because a good portion of the people that were considered 'missing' have shown up after the alleged disappearances."

Alex stared at him in confusion. "I don't understand."

KENZO

Frank kicked his feet out in front of him and crossed his legs by the ankles. "There was a guy named Ted. His coworker said that he was supposed to come over one night and never showed up. Didn't turn up to work for the next five days but then a few people saw him running around Brewster on a few different occasions. Multiple eyewitnesses. Why you askin'?"

Alex sighed heavily as she joined him and sank into the seat opposite him. "Last night this reporter, Rachel, dropped by my apartment to talk to me about the disappearances and the animal running around."

"Of course she did." Frank rolled his eyes. "Yeah, you should stop listening to the rubbish that she says. In-person and in the newspaper. She's just trying to make things sound more interesting than they actually are, giving Henry a hell of a time, too. She thinks that the missing people are part of some conspiracy, that this animal is doing more damage and Henry is covering it up. Truth is some of the missing people that Rachel wants to pin this theory on aren't exactly missing. She's reaching now but I'm afraid she might work people up into a frenzy. People don't like rational explanations when they're locked on their irrational ones."

Alex understood that. Her disdain for Rachel was growing. Frank pulled out his phone and checked it before shoving it back into his pants with an annoyed sound.

"What's wrong?" Alex asked.

"It's Charlie. I tried to talk to him after we saw him that day but he still won't pick up the phone. I don't know why."

"Maybe he's just hiding from Victor."

"I don't know but I don't like it. Been leaving him those messages and it's not like him not to answer."

"Well, there's not much you can do there apart from going to his house and confronting him."

Frank's eyes shone. "There's an idea."

"But, you can't go now." She said as he walked to the door. He threw up his hands with a strangled sigh. "Fine. After this shift."

They opened up to the usual flood of customers and had fallen into their routine with Alex manning the till and the tables while Frank spent his time obsessively checking his watch and his phone intermittently.

It was around midday when Detectives David and Henry strolled into the coffee shop. Frank rolled his eyes to the ceiling. "We don't have doughnuts today." He called out.

"Funny." Henry snapped. He looked up at Alex and she shied away behind the counter. "Good afternoon," he called out.

"Hi," Alex mumbled back. What did they want now? Has someone else gone missing?

Henry seemed to know what she was thinking because he answered her unspoken question almost immediately. He handed her a picture of a man.

"Remember how we asked you if you saw a man named Grant Nichols?"

"Yeah." She said reluctantly.

"Still haven't seen him?"

Alex shook her head.

"So, he wasn't who you saw a few nights ago?"

"I didn't see anyone. Not really. I just saw movement."

Henry nodded. "Fine." He looked over at his brother. "Frank, how about you?"

"Haven't seen that idiot since you last asked me. I'm sure he will turn up though. Might've been something prowling around out there but I can't imagine him going hiking in the woods so I'd say he's safe."

To that, Alex had to agree, but Henry and David did have a job to do.

Henry and David left shortly after they arrived, carrying their pastries and cups of coffee out the door with them. Frank sent them off with a lazy salute and Henry returned it with less than civil parting words.

As closing time came, Frank seemed to become more antsy and they ended up closing a few minutes earlier.

"I can drop you off before I go see Charlie." Frank offered.

Alex shook her head. Frank had taken to giving her a ride home after her shift seeing as the walk was so long and the evenings had gotten pretty dark. "It's fine. You said you just wanted to check up on him."

"Right. shouldn't take too long. Shift's over. Let's close up."

They climbed into his truck and began the drive to Charlie's home. He took 'the scenic' route. Alex was starting to fall asleep in her seat when she heard him swear under his breath.

Her eyes snapped open and she saw what he was staring at.

A dark-haired, lanky, man walked along the pavement ahead of them, as they drove by. She remembered him from the first time she had met Frank. He had passed her on the way out of *The Hideaway*.

Frank rolled down his window and yelled out of it. "Oi, Charlie."

The man named Charlie didn't look around, even as others who presumably weren't named Charlie did.

Alex looked back at Frank, who looked shocked and pissed at the same time. He swore again and pulled the truck to the curb before he jumped out.

"That bastard!" He hissed.

"Do you actually know that guy?" She called after him. "I mean, are you sure that's your friend and not someone else?" She joked.

"Hell, yeah I'm sure!" He yelled back. "And that bastard has been ignoring me for days!"

Amused, Alex jumped out of the truck, behind him and struggled to keep up.

She rushed behind Frank as he strode purposefully down the street after his friend. Ahead of them, the back of the man's head bobbed along, weaving in and out of the crowds.

"Wait a minute," Alex called out to Frank.

Frank flicked her a glance over his shoulder but kept his brisk pace. He was considerably taller than her and his legs reached further than hers did. There was also the fact that Frank didn't seem too deterred by the cars he crossed in front of.

Alex scurried behind him as quickly as she could, praying that her job wouldn't always end up with her running after Frank. She began wishing that she hadn't left with him and just found her way home. She was tired and getting hungry. And if she lost Frank, she wouldn't know how to get home from here.

When she woke up in the morning she never thought that she would have been so desperate to still be at work.

"Frank," she hissed again, after the honk of a car horn ripped through the air in front of them. "Let's go back to the truck, you can talk to him later."

Frank shot her a blazing look over his shoulder as they walked. "I've been calling that bastard all week, thinking that the fool tripped and broke his neck or something, and that prick walks by me, happy as a clam and don't even have the manners to turn around."

Ahead of them the man in question turned onto another street and disappeared around a corner. Frank picked up speed, with Alex struggling to keep pace.

As they reached the end of the street, Alex saw that their target had disappeared into the crowd of people coming and going along the street.

"Shit." Frank cursed loudly.

The stitch in Alex's side pulsed unhelpfully as she searched the sparse crowd with Frank.

"Why...why don't we just wait outside his door? You know where he lives, right? Let's just do that." Alex wheezed.

Frank looked down at her curiously. "Yeah, let's do that." He muttered absently. He turned and walked back the way they had come, with Alex trailing along resentfully behind him. "We'll wait for that bastard to show his face. Then he can explain what he's playing at."

Frank's long strides led him to his truck first, far ahead of Alex, while Alex's stitch, her reluctance and annoyance brought her back a minute after he arrived. When she climbed into the passenger seat next to him, he was tapping the wheel impatiently.

"You dragging your feet?"

"We just saw him go that way," Alex panted, pointing behind her in the general direction their target had gone. "We'll get there way before he does." She slammed the door shut behind her.

"Yeah, well I'm impatient. Now buckle up."

Frank started his truck and pulled away from the curb as Alex rushed to lock her seatbelt in place.

They sped down the road, dodging honking cars and making sharp turns every so often. While Alex wasn't an expert on the layout of Kenzo, she was beginning to recognise the areas they passed through. They had started in Brewster and were heading towards Brighthall.

They had barely parked when Frank yanked off his seatbelt and marched down the road to his friend's house.

Alex rushed behind him and failed to notice when he stopped abruptly outside of the closed door. She leaned around him to see what had caught his attention, but she couldn't see anything past Frank.

"Frank," she called to him tentatively. She placed a hand on his elbow and tried to turn him to face her. He let her move him and nodded his head to the handle.

Alex craned her neck and saw that there was a red smudge on the brass handle.

Alex took a step back and pulled him with her. He allowed her to move them a step before he stepped forward and kicked his heel against the door. The force of his foot broke the door open and Frank moved forwards, cautiously, as he called out to his friend. Frank moved from room to room with purpose, his eyes scanning the room before he left it for the next one.

Alex looked around to see if anyone had noticed Frank's unlawful entry, but as far as she could tell no one had seen anything.

She slipped in through the broken doorway and whispered to Frank. "Just wait."

"For what?"

"Your brother. Let's call him and get him to deal with this."

Frank scoffed at her before he rounded out of the living room and stormed into the kitchen. Alex followed him, making sure that she didn't touch anything, or leave a significant trail that could come back to bite her.

"You smell that?" He asked softly. There was a pungent odour wafting through the room. It made her nose wrinkle.

Alex nodded. "Yeah," she whispered back. "More reason for us to call Henry."

Frank stalked around the kitchen until his eyes landed on a door.

"That's the basement." He muttered.

He looked to her for confirmation, but Alex didn't know why. He hadn't listened to her so far, but she gave him a small nod. The further they went, the stronger the smell got.

Frank opened the door and out wafted the overwhelming rancid stench of rotting meat. Both Alex and Frank gagged, and Frank slammed the door shut. The two of them shared a look before Frank pushed the door open again.

Behind the door was the dark open space of the basement. Frank flicked on the light and a feeble glow emanated from the bulb in the middle of the room. It didn't do much to chase away the dark, but it allowed them to see in front of them.

Frank descended the steps first with Alex close behind him. Once their feet touched the ground, they looked around at the dark empty basement.

As their eyes struggled to adjust to the dark, for a moment, Alex was brought back to the night she arrived in Kenzo. The same fear she had felt standing outside in the cold crept up her arms and legs, threatening to swallow her whole. The faint buzzing of flies grew louder as they approached. Alex knew what they would find, she had since they arrived at Charlie's doorstep, but still, they continued.

They looked around and their eyes were drawn to a dark mass in the back of the room.

Frank stood frozen where he was, but Alex moved forwards, almost unconsciously.

In the corner of the room sat the remains of a man, his neck twisted at an unnatural angle, as flies and maggots swarmed in and around him.

"Charlie." Frank croaked.

CHAPTER 14

Alex and Frank stood staring for a few minutes. This was the man they had just seen out on the street, and now he was dead. From the smell of his body, he'd been dead for quite some time before they had even arrived.

But how was that possible?

Alex turned to Frank. He stood staring at the body in front of them. Alex pulled on his sleeve and drew his attention again. As his eyes rolled up to meet hers, she started guiding them back to the stairs.

"Frank, are you sure that was Charlie you saw out there?"

Frank stumbled with her until they reached the bottom step and then he nodded. "Yeah, it was him."

"Are you sure?" Alex repeated. She had no idea what was going on, but they would need to figure it out before they could call anyone. "Maybe the guy just looked like him."

"No," Frank murmured stubbornly.

"We only saw him as we passed. We only really saw his back."

Frank shook his head and pulled his arm away from her. "You've never actually met him, but I've known him for years. He's worn the same damn coat for the past fourteen. I know what he looks like."

Charlie's coat.

Alex rushed up the stairs. She could hear Frank scramble up them after her, though she wasn't sure if that was out of concern for her, or if he didn't want to be left alone in the basement with his dead friend.

She supposed both were valid reasons, either way.

"Where would he keep his coat? Do you know?" Alex asked as she searched through the house, looking for any coats or shoes that might be lying around.

"He has a coat stand by the door."

Both he and Alex headed straight for it. The coat stand was next to the front door, just as Frank had said, and it only held a scarf that had been wrapped around it. They both stopped at the same time, and Alex could tell that they had come to the same conclusion.

"Coat's gone."

Alex nodded numbly.

Charlie was downstairs, and the coat was gone. But what did that prove? Frank had said that he had seen Charlie, wearing the same coat he always had and it was missing from the stand here. But what did that prove? Alex had been there and even she felt doubt. How would they explain this to anyone else?

Because Charlie was dead, and something was walking around in his coat if not Charlie himself.

Before Alex had a chance to open her mouth and voice her questions and her fears, Frank had pulled his phone out of his pocket and begun dialling.

"Are you calling Henry?" She whispered.

Frank nodded. "He should be able to figure this out." When Henry answered at the other end, Alex searched through the house one more time, while Frank explained the situation.

From what she could tell, the windows and doors hadn't been forced, save for the front door they had kicked in.

Frank got off the phone and found Alex in the kitchen where she was staring at the back door.

"You think he got in through there?" He asked her, gesturing towards the backdoor.

Alex shook her head. "No. He didn't force it."

"You think Charlie let him in?"

"Maybe, but I doubt that too. I have no idea, but I think the important thing is to explain to Henry what we saw."

"I agree."

"But..." Alex began, turning around to face him. "We have to find a way of saying this without sounding crazy."

Frank was silent for a moment. "I saw him." He answered finally.

"But you couldn't have." Alex sighed and dragged a hand over her face. "I believe you, I was there. But do you think that Henry will believe that you saw the guy alive and a few minutes later, you found his rotting body?"

Frank remained silent. He glanced down at his phone and then back up at her. "We only mention the body. I'll say I was looking for him and we came here before I was gonna drop you off home."

Alex nodded. "Okay."

They both stood in silence for the next twenty minutes, as they waited for Henry and David to arrive.

When they did, both Frank and Alex heard Henry swear under his breath, as he pushed the broken door open.

"In here," Frank called, as he walked out of the kitchen, with Alex on his heels. As they walked through the hallway, they saw both Henry and David standing at the front door.

"What the hell is this?" Henry asked, pointing at the door behind them. The lock was hanging on to the door by a screw.

"It was locked," Frank muttered. "Had to get in some way."

"Did you, now?"

"Look, I was worried about my friend, and I had a right to be. There was blood on the doorknob."

Henry looked from Frank to Alex. "Where's he?"

Alex pointed her finger behind her. "He's in the basement." She turned and led the group back to the kitchen.

Henry took the lead and pushed open the door, with Alex and Frank behind him and David at the back.

When they all stood in front of Charlie's corpse, no one spoke or did anything for a few minutes. With a sigh, David stepped forwards and crouched down next to the body. "Looks like he's been dead for a while." His nose

wrinkled at the smell. "When's the last time you saw him?"
He said to Frank.

Frank shrugged. "I hadn't heard from him for a while.
That's why I got worried."

"So, you just decided to visit?" Henry asked. His eyes
moved from Frank to Alex and back. "The two of you?"

"I was dropping her home."

Henry scoffed. "That's a ways away."

Frank turned to look at Henry incredulously. "Yeah, we
were getting there." He snapped. "I just wanted to check
on my friend first."

"Just like that?"

"Yeah, just like that! You got something to say, Henry?
Say it!"

Both Henry and Frank glared at each other. David
stood up. "It looks like his neck was broken. There are
some scratch marks, too." He announced.

Everyone looked at him, and then at the body. In the
dim light, it was hard to be sure of anything, but Charlie's
body was sat on a chair, his head slouched over. If it wasn't
for the smell and the flies, he could have been sleeping.
But, as Alex tilted her head, she could see that his neck was
swollen and bent at an odd angle. There were also long

scratches as if whatever had killed him had long nails. They couldn't be sure, but it was clear that Charlie didn't die naturally.

"You get into any trouble recently?" Henry asked abruptly.

Frank snorted a laugh. "No, and neither had he." He nodded to Charlie.

Henry dragged a hand over his beard. His eyes snapped to Alex. "Start from the beginning. What happened?"

Warily, Alex retold her day at work with Frank. She explained every small mundane detail carefully until they reached the part where they had seen Charlie. It was there that she stumbled in her recount, and she could tell that Henry had noticed.

"When we were finished locking up, Frank offered to drop me home. And then...we, on the way, he said that you know, he wanted to see a friend, because he erm, hadn't seen for a while, so..."

She looked up and saw Henry glaring down at her. At first, she thought that he was angry at her, but then she saw his eyes move to his brother. "Ok," He said finally. He turned to David. "Call it in. Take him with you." He nodded at Frank.

When the two of them had left, and Henry and Alex were alone, Henry turned back to Alex. "What happened after you two locked up?"

Alex shrugged. "Frank wanted-"

"Alex." He warned. "What happened?"

"Frank wanted to meet his friend." That was true.

"Why didn't he drop you off first?"

Alex shrugged again. She looked at the body in the corner and then back at Henry. "He hadn't seen him in a while, and he said that he wanted to check on him."

Henry stared at her silently. Alex stared back, trying to read his eyes. He was suspicious, clearly, but he seemed suspicious of both of them.

He knew they were hiding something, and it was the dishonesty that was causing him to scrutinise them.

Maybe, the truth was needed.

"Look," she began, "when we were driving to *Cassandra's*, we saw him, Charlie, on the road. Frank tried to call out to him, but he didn't answer. We tried to chase him, and he didn't turn around. So, I suggested that we go to his house to wait for him if that's what Frank wanted. When we got here there was blood on the handle like Frank said, so he broke down the door, and we found him here. I asked Frank if he was sure that it was his friend he saw outside, and he was positive, the guy was even wearing his coat. The coat's normally on the coat rack, and it's not here, so..." Alex took a deep breath, "I think that maybe, whoever did this, is the same person that we saw outside."

Throughout her whole confession, Henry had barely moved and Alex wondered if he believed anything she had said, but then he shifted and the intensity in his eyes boiled down.

"Frank saw him?" He muttered softly.

Alex eyed him carefully. "Yeah. We didn't think you'd believe us. Well, I didn't."

Henry's jaw clenched and his eyes became distant. "Yeah, well, I've seen some strange things." He murmured.

"Like what?"

Henry shook his head. "It doesn't matter."

"Do you think it's connected to the other murders?"

Henry shrugged his large shoulders. "Too soon to tell."

As he turned to leave, a thought burrowed its way into Alex's head and once it was there, it took root. A small hunch, that was shifting her perspective.

KENZO

"I saw something strange the night you found me at the bus stop."

Henry stopped in his tracks but didn't turn around.

"Whatever was in the bushes wasn't a person I saw. It was something else. And it was watching me."

Alex knew that what she had seen that night wasn't a person, no matter what was said. But there were very few people who would believe her and take her words seriously. People who hadn't seen what she had seen.

For a moment, Henry didn't move or speak, but she knew he had heard her. After a long pause, he spoke finally.

"I'll drop you home." He muttered, before trudging up the stairs, each step creaking under his weight.

It was then that Alex knew that her hunch had been correct.

Henry may not know what was prowling around Kenzo, but he didn't think it was human any more than she did.

He knew that whatever it was, it was not a human or an animal.

During the ride home, both Alex and Frank had remained silent, heavy with the weight of what they had seen.

Charlie has been dead for a while at least two weeks, she would say but they had seen him just the day before.

How is that possible?

Alex knew that's exactly what Frank was thinking too. She could almost see the cogs in his head turning.

She spent the rest of the night lying down in bed staring at the ceiling, wondering just how and why Frank's friend had ended up dead.

Alex only realised it was morning once again when she noticed the sun shining in through her windows. Her curtains were flimsy enough that they allowed the pale light to come in.

It was still dark outside but light enough that she knew that dawn was breaking.

Distantly she heard the sound of footsteps padding through the hallway and a key fumbling for a lock.

Alex bolted up in her bed. She needed answers and she realised that she could get them from Spencer.

She jumped up from her bed and ran through her apartment until she reached her front door. As she yanked it open, she caught a glimpse of Spencer just as he had turned to close his door. He looked up at her in surprise.

"Alex?" he said slowly. His voice sounded thick with sleep and his eyes had dark circles under them.

"They called you didn't they? Henry and David? About Charlie?"

Spencer's eyes narrowed and nodded once. "But, I can't tell you anything."

Alex scoffed. "Are you kidding me? You can't honestly think I had anything to do with what happened to him! Me or Frank! We both found him. I just want to know what happened."

"I can't tell you anything."

"You can't tell me? Now, is that because I'm a civilian and I'm not allowed to know police business or because I'm a suspect? Or is it because I'm not your nosey neighbour living upstairs?"

Spencer tensed at the mention of Goldie.

"Because you seem to have no trouble talking to her about things. Strange, considering she can't seem to keep her mouth shut."

Spencer looked at his feet, uncomfortable. "I didn't tell her-"

"You told her enough. Goldie's been avoiding me. And so have you. Any idea why that might be?"

Spencer blanched. "What? I don't...look, I'm sorry but right now we don't know much."

"Then tell me what you do know."

Spencer sighed heavily. "He's been dead for at least a few weeks. It looks like his neck was snapped. No sign that anyone broke in, according to the detectives. They say that you and Frank saw him yesterday."

Alex nodded. "Yeah, we did."

"Well, you couldn't have because he definitely didn't die yesterday."

"We know. That's what's been puzzling us." Alex frowned at the floor before she looked back up at him. "Do you think I had anything to do with this?"

Spencer's expression became guarded but he shook his head. "No. I don't see why you would do this and I don't see how you'll be able to. You're too small."

"Well, what about what happened with Marcia?"

Spencer rubbed his eyes behind his glasses. "I don't think you did that either, to be honest. Both murders required a lot of upper body strength or at least, height, and sorry, but I don't think you have either."

Alex nodded. "Ok, can you tell Goldie? She tried to dodge me, just as I was coming in. I'd rather my name not be connected to a crime, to help make sure that my neighbours didn't all think I was a serial killer." She muttered, almost to herself, as she walked back to her apartment, slamming the door shut behind her.

CHAPTER 15

The sun had barely begun to crest over the horizon when there was a knock at the door.

Alex had been lying in bed, staring at the cracked ceiling, wondering just how much further this was going to escalate.

She had hoped that just being vigilant and sticking to well-lit and crowded streets would be enough that she would never have to worry about this creature again.

That wasn't true.

She had gone over everything again and again in her head, waiting for everything to make sense, but with every minute that passed a new thought would enter her head, and she would be faced with more questions. She had gone to bed physically worn out, but with her mind racing. Her mind had whirled for the past few hours, trying to understand how they had found the decaying corpse of a man they had seen alive and well only an hour before. She hadn't realised that she had gone through the night without closing her eyes once until she heard the knock at the door.

Alex padded into her living room and perched on her couch, listening and waiting.

She didn't think it was a good idea to open the door this early since she wasn't expecting anyone and considering recent events, it was dangerous.

A few beats went past before there was another knock at the door, but this time it was accompanied by a voice.

"Alex? It's me. We need to talk."

That was Frank. Alex stood up and walked to her front door. She rose up on her toes and pressed her eye to the peephole. In the hallway stood Frank. He looked antsy, shifting on his feet as he looked around him.

Alex pulled back, and yawning, she opened her front door. She stepped aside, allowing him into her apartment. "What did you want to talk about?" She mumbled as she rubbed her tired eyes.

Frank strolled into her living room and turned to face her incredulously. "Like you don't know. Charlie, of course. Unless you want to talk about the weather."

Alex rubbed her eyes. "You know more than I do about him." She admitted as she locked the door behind him. "I just have to take your word for it."

She walked to the couch and collapsed on top of it as Frank glared at her impatiently.

"I've been thinking about what we saw." He started.

"Really? I couldn't tell."

Frank stopped his pacing to shoot her a glare. "Really not in the mood for jokes, right now."

Alex held up a hand. "Sorry, go on."

"That couldn't be Charlie, right? We saw him walking around. You saw him."

Alex opened her mouth to agree but she paused. Frank was the one who knew Charlie. Alex had never even met him.

Frank would be the one with more answers than her. He seemed to come to the same conclusion as he tutted in irritation and turned away from her. He started to pace, rubbing his stubbled cheek as he did. Alex watched him curiously, as the cogs turned in his head. This wasn't something he didn't already know, but Alex knew that he hadn't come for information.

He had come for confirmation.

He wanted things to make sense in his head, and he needed someone who would listen to his mad theories without dismissing them as soon as they left his mouth. Alex knew the feeling all too well since it had kept her up all night. She too needed someone to explain the situation to her, but she wouldn't push him.

He would tell her when he was ready. So Alex sat in silence, watching as Frank's mind continued to whirl.

After a few minutes of silence, Frank turned back to her. "We saw him outside."

"I know." She agreed.

"It was him. I know it was." Frank's voice was uncertain, even in his conviction.

She had only glimpsed Charlie once while he was alive, seen his decayed face in the dark basement and seen the back of the head of a man Frank was sure was his friend.

She was going by what Frank had said, not from actual evidence and from the frantic look on Frank's face, he wouldn't want to hear that right now.

"Don't doubt yourself." She answered finally. "If you saw him, I believe you. I've seen some crazy things before."

Frank scoffed humorlessly and he raised his eyes to the ceiling. "And how the fuck did he die? When? Why? Why him? He's an idiot but most people like him. None of this makes fucking sense."

Alex clasped her hands together and squeezed her fingers. "There's a boy who lives in this building. He thinks that the people going missing are being murdered. He thinks there's an animal that's responsible for all of it." She looked down at her hands. "I think I believe him."

Frank stared at her, puzzled. "What do you mean? That all that stuff is related? The animal attacks and the missing people? I doubt it."

"Why?"

"Because they didn't just disappear. I told you! I even saw the first guy that 'went missing', Matt Brooks, last Wednesday."

Three sharp knocks on the front door made both Alex and Frank jump at the noise.

The knocks repeated and this time it was accompanied by the sharp, clear, persistent voice of Alex's least favourite reporter.

"Hello? Alex? It's Rachel Ellis. Can I talk to you for a moment?"

Frank rolled his eyes to the ceiling "Just fuckin' great."

Alex jerked her head towards the door in question. Frank scowled petulantly but nodded once.

Reluctantly Alex walked back to her door and yanked it open. On the other side was the inquisitive reporter. Her eyes moved from Alex to Frank. "Oh, good, I'm glad I found both of you."

"I bet you are," Frank mumbled.

Rachel shifted where she stood and refocused on Alex, clearly assuming her to be the more sympathetic one. She would be wrong if she thought so.

Alex had been linked to a few too many less-than-legal incidents that drew too much attention to her.

And she had Rachel to thank for some of that.

"I heard that the two of you were at Charlie Hitchman's home when he was found dead."

"Yeah, what about it?" Frank snapped.

Rachel glanced at him warily and reached her hand into her handbag and pulled out a tape recorder. "Would you mind giving me a statement about what you saw?"

Frank marched forward and placed himself between Rachel and Alex. "We would mind, as it happens."

Rachel turned back to Alex, leaning around Frank's intimidating frame to look into her eyes. "Alex, how about you?"

Alex took a step away from Rachel, and Frank's posture relaxed. "We've both had a long day and Charlie was a good friend of Frank's, so it's still a bit sore for him right now. Besides, don't you have enough to do with your other article?'

Rachel sighed and put away her tape recorder. "Look, I'm just trying to help."

Frank rolled his eyes. "Help who, exactly? Because it sure as shit won't help Charlie. It won't help us."

"You'll hear this soon, but it looks like Charlie's been dead for at least a week."

For a second, neither Alex nor Frank said anything, but Alex could feel the simmering rage boiling up in him.

"No." He said, shaking his head. "No."

Alex didn't want to upset Frank any more than he already had been but she needed to know. With a glance at Frank, she asked the question that had been on her mind since they found Charlie "How did he die?"

Rachel gave Frank a quick cursory glance before she answered as delicately as someone as blunt and invasive as

Rachel could. "His neck was broken with extreme force. The coroners don't know what was responsible for it, but they know that he was placed in his chair a few hours after his death."

Charlie's neck had been twisted at an angle, That had been something that Alex remembered vividly, that and the smell of Charlie suffocating them in the basement.

"If you could tell me about anything you saw."

This time Alex interjected before Frank could even open his mouth. "Are you seriously still searching for another story?"

"I wanted to talk to Charlie about Marie."

"What? Why?"

"Perhaps now isn't the best time."

She turned towards the front door, but Alex blocked her. "It hasn't been 'the best time' since you got here, but that didn't stop you before."

Rachel sighed and took a deep breath. "I wanted to ask Charlie about Marie's disappearance."

"Why?" Frank murmured. "You're writing about missing people. What's that got to do with Charlie?"

Rachel hesitated but raised her head and continued. "He might have heard something."

"Heard what?"

"I can't tell you much right now, just that there may be some overlap in the cases."

"What do you know?"

Rachel pressed her lips together. "I'm sorry, I can't say." She stepped past Alex, opened the front door and slipped out. "I'll talk to you soon." She called behind her.

Alex and Frank stood in silence for a minute before Alex marched to the couch, she sank down onto the cushions and drummed her fingers.

The noise drew Frank's scowl. "What are you doing?"

Alex shifted on the couch to give Frank space to sit. "Sit down."

Frank looked tempted to ignore her, but finally, he obeyed. "What now?"

"If Rachel thinks she figured something out, maybe she did."

"Like what?"

"She's been looking into Marie's disappearance. Remember what I was saying before Rachel showed up? That the disappearances could be connected. You said something about Matt something.

"Matt Brooks." He mumbled.

"Yeah, you said..." He had said that he had seen Matt long after he had been assumed missing. "You've seen him since his official disappearance, right?"

"Heard he went missing about a year ago, but I didn't think anything of it, cause I saw him walking around."

"What if it wasn't him?"

"What do you mean?"

"We saw Charlie walking around, the same day we found him. He was dead for at least a week. Matt was missing, but you saw him walking around."

Frank dragged a hand over his face. "You think something is...what, impersonating people? That's ridiculous."

"Can you explain what you saw then?"

"I know what I saw, but that is...no one would believe us."

"That's fine, we just have to start somewhere."

CHAPTER 16

A few days had passed since Charlie's corpse was found, but the events surrounding it hadn't become any clearer. Frank and Alex had tried to make sense of it, whenever they had spare time, but weren't any closer to figuring out what had happened.

It didn't help that Goldie had still been actively avoiding Alex, whenever she saw her in the halls, choosing to go back up the stairs she had come down, or outright walk past her.

Alex almost didn't see Rachel standing outside her apartment. She was too busy thinking of Goldie's strange behaviour to notice when the woman took a step towards her and almost ran into her.

"Hi," Rachel offered tentatively. "I came by to speak with you. Do you have a moment to spare?"

Alex eyed her warily as she fidgeted with the keys in her hand. She was wearing a green raincoat, with a messenger bag over her shoulder. "I can see that, but no. Not right now." Alex answered back acidly. She had nothing but spare time, but none of it she wanted to spend talking to Rachel.

"Please? Just a few questions and I'll go."

"Fine," Alex said reluctantly. She stepped past Rachel and unlocked her door. The woman followed her inside and looked around before she perched on the seat of the couch.

Alex put down her backpack wearily and threw her keys onto the coffee table.

"Have the detective mentioned anything to you about Marcia?"

"No. They haven't."

"So, are you a suspect?"

"No."

"But they spoke to you first about it." Clearly, she hadn't let that go.

Alex felt her jaw flex and her teeth grind together. "They heard that I had spoken with Marcia a few days before she died." The memory of the supermarket came flooding back to Alex, and she felt a surge of anger rise inside of her. "Yeah, they heard that I had an altercation with her in the supermarket."

"What kind of altercation?" Rachel asked curiously.

Alex scowled down at her fingers. "Marcia had gotten the idea that I knew something about her daughter. That I might be able to help her." Alex looked up at Rachel from beneath her eyelashes. "She said that you told her I knew something."

Rachel's eyes widened in surprise. "I didn't say that exactly."

"Well, what did you say? Because she thought that I could help her find her daughter. She thought that as a girl who lived on the street, I would have run into her or something like that. She said that you said so."

Rachel's eyes flickered in confusion. "I told her about our conversation after she left the parking lot of Freddie's. I just told her that perhaps we can get a better perspective of how Marie might have felt, and why she might have gone off in the first place. I didn't mean that you could find her."

"Well, I don't think you made that clear enough to her, because she grabbed me in the middle of a supermarket. Everyone saw me shout at her. That's why they talked to me." Alex wondered why a reporter like Rachel wouldn't already know all of this. She had been helping Marcia after all.

"I am so sorry for any distress I might have put you through. That was not my intention when I spoke to her. I was just trying to help comfort her, help her get into the mindset of someone who might run away. I thought that might help."

"I don't think it did." Alex snapped. "Because a few hours later she ended up dead."

Rachel looked uncomfortable. She reached into her bag and took out a notepad and a pen. "Could you...?"

"No!" Alex put up a hand. "Look, I don't normally talk to reporters, so if this is just for another one of your articles, you can just leave, because I don't want any trouble. I don't want my name in anything!"

"We're not the bad guys, you know. We're just trying to help."

"So far, it doesn't seem like you're helping anyone but yourself."

Rachel frowned. "I spoke to one of your neighbours, Marigold Samson, and she seems to be concerned about you."

"Yeah, I noticed." Alex cut in.

"Apparently, someone...a friend of hers had told her a few things."

"Let me guess...a 'friend' told her what little he knew, and she ran with that. Great." Alex muttered. "Look, I don't really have anything else interesting to add. I don't know anything, I didn't see anything. I don't even know anyone. I really wish people would stop thinking that I know more than I do. Because I don't! And, to be honest, I'm not sure I want to know. I just want to mind my own business and move along with my life, so if there's nothing else..." Alex trailed off, impatiently waiting for Rachel to catch on.

Rachel relented and got up from her seat. "Fine. Elise Chambers was a well-known therapist who used to live in Belamour. Messy divorce from her husband and she ended up here in Troye. She went for a hike one day and didn't come back home. Then two weeks later her body was found, mauled by an animal."

"Why are you telling me this?"

"My articles are just to make sure that Kenzo can be a safe place where things like this didn't happen. Like it was before. Within the past year, there have been multiple disappearances, multiple deaths and no one can explain why, or even how they're happening."

She reached into her bag and pulled out a notebook and began to read the scrawl on the page.

"Matt Brooks went missing January 6th 1994. A few months after, Malcolm Walker was found dead, on April 18th, an animal attack. Dylan Lindsay was found on May 9th. Another animal attack. Doug Armstrong went missing on July 9th. Connie Simmons, September 13th. Missing. Bethany Shin, November 17th. Missing. Elise Chambers died from an animal attack on December 22nd. Grant Nichols, January 4th 1995. Missing. And just recently a woman named Claire Hawkins was found dead from an animal attack on February 23rd. The first to go missing was Marie Rosen. She disappeared January 1st 1994."

Alex folded her arms over her chest. "Why do you think they're all related? The animal attacks, sure, but the missing people might be unrelated."

"I didn't think there was a connection at first. My article was just supposed to be about the rising crime in Kenzo. But, the more I researched into this, the more I knew something was not right. After Marie Rosen, the number of missing people in Kenzo increased, with no explanation. And then there were the animal attacks. The attacks are being done by some sort of animal, at least according to the police and animal control, but no one's seen it. No one even knows for sure what kind of creature it might be. Just speculation. And it's impossible to track."

Alex shrugged. "That's what they say. No reason not to believe them."

"But, what if it's not an animal? What if someone is using that to cover something up?"

"Sounds a bit far-fetched." Alex raised an eyebrow. "Any ideas?"

Rachel's eyes narrowed. "Before he died, Charlie wanted to talk to me. He didn't say what about but now he's dead and..." She trailed off. "Something needs to be done. If more people hear the truth then maybe something can be done to prevent another death."

"You think Marie's got something to do with the animal attacks?"

Rachel shrugged. "Could be."

"Do you think that Marcia's death had something to do with that woman, Elise Chambers?"

"It might do. A lot of things aren't adding up."

Alex shrugged. "I'm sorry. I still don't know how I can help. I'm not an animal catcher or a people catcher."

Rachel nodded. "I understand. But if you see anything, you will call me, won't you?"

"I will." Alex would promise anything to get Rachel out of her apartment. She knew the other woman was onto something, but that was best explored without her.

Rachel nodded again and stood. "You still have my card?"

"Yeah, and even if I didn't, you know where to find me."

Rachel gave her a wry smile. "I do so, until then." She opened the door and left.

Alex waited for a moment before she locked it behind her. She didn't want to seem too eager to get the woman out of her apartment, but she had no desire to speak to Rachel again.

She still didn't trust Rachel's motives and even if she had the purest of intentions, Alex didn't see how that would stop a vicious monster from rampaging through the streets of Kenzo.

She had been surprised to find out that Goldie had spoken to Rachel about her, and that she had been concerned enough about Alex that she had talked to the reporter although considering Goldie's habit of talking, non-stop, even to strangers, that probably didn't mean much.

Rachel probably had asked for a few questions and that had led to Goldie spewing the first few thoughts that had crossed her mind. But she had been told by Spencer that Alex was considered a suspect in the investigation.

Was this before or after he had spoken to her at *The Hideaway?* He seemed suspicious of her then. Had he already confided his suspicions to Goldie out of fear of Alex or had he just told his friend a piece of information? He didn't seem to think of Alex as a suspect. She had spoken to him but it proved that he had been concerned about her as a stranger in their building. She didn't blame him, to be honest, but since she had done nothing wrong the suspicion was inconvenient.

There was no motive for her to kill. She had just come into town and had no motive for wanting to kill anyone. Not seriously. Not enough to go through with it.

There was a knock at the door. Alex froze where she stood for a second before she tiptoed back toward the door. She peaked through the peephole and saw Rachel standing outside. Her shoulder bag had been put away, but still had her green raincoat.

Automatically, she opened the door. "Yeah?" she answered.

Rachel grimaced. "I'm sorry to do this, but there are a few more questions that I wanted to ask you, that completely slipped my mind."

Alex tensed again. "OK, like what?"

"When you were at the bus stop, did you see anything?"

"What?" Alex asked surprised.

"I mean they found remains near the bus stop and they said you were nearby so, I just want to know if you saw anything there. Anyone?"

Alex thought back to the night that she had been stranded. She remembered the cold that had seeped into her fingers and the fear of seeing the eyes buried between the branches of the trees.

"No, I didn't."

Rachel grimaced. "Are you sure? Because I heard that you saw someone there. That's what you told the police. You sent them out there to investigate."

Alex frowned again. "Who told you this?"

"The detectives. They said you saw something. You must have seen the animal that was going around Kenzo since the remains were close by. You must have stumbled onto it. It sounds like you had a lucky escape. I just want to know what you saw."

"Well, I didn't see much. I think the police would know more than I do."

'Do you know what kind of creature it is?"

Alex frowned again. "I saw a person. "She said remembering what she had told Detective Lovett and Detective Li. It had been a lie, but that was what her story had been. Why was Rachel so adamant that she had seen an animal?

"Fine." Rachel relented. "I'm sorry to bother you. I know that you've had a hard few days. It's not easy adjusting to a new area especially when you feel everyone is out to get you."

Alex gave a small nod. "Yeah."

Rachel smiled again, but this one seems more pulled than her previous ones. "The detectives are trying their best, but between you and me, I think everyone would be better off watching their own backs. The police can't be everywhere, you know?"

"No."

Rachel smiled again and she walked away. "See you." She called over her shoulder.

"See you," answered Alex as she closed the door and locked it behind her.

She wasn't sure what Rachel's angle was but she knew that she had no intention of leaving her alone.

As she walked to the shower, she resolved to look into the cases herself. Perhaps ask Frank for some help seeing as he was the only person who didn't recoil from her or make her feel like she was under a heavy spotlight every time they ask her a question.

She left her apartment and headed for the bus stop. She walked quickly through the misty streets with a plan to pick Frank's brain for everything that he knew.

As a brother of a detective and more specifically the detective on the case that had baffled everyone.

No, he must know things that the general public might not, just like how Spencer had told Goldie, perhaps Henry Lovett had confided in his brother, Frank about the case he was working on.

Rachel had a point that there were an alarming amount of disappearances and animal attacks that had occurred recently and that someone should look into it but from what Alex understood David and Henry were doing their best. They just had no idea that the animal that was prowling around was supernatural.

Alex had been avoiding the topic. She had wanted to admit it to herself and hoped that she had escaped such things and was just in a nice normal town with normal people and animals.

At the time she had seen the creature, she was in no position to worry about anything but herself and days after that.

She had to worry about her new environment, getting a job and fitting into a strange place but now she had time to slow down, she realised just how much damage was being done by the monster roaming Kenzo.

CHAPTER 17

When Frank unlocked his front door and let Alex into his home, Alex couldn't help but notice how tired he looked.

She had called him right after Rachel's second visit, and he had come over and driven her to his place.

She stepped inside and looked around at the warm welcoming interior, which made hers look so cold by comparison. It looked like a family home, trapped in another time. It didn't look like it belonged to Frank at all.

"Don't get too comfy. Henry's picking us up for dinner."

"Really? Us?"

Frank picked up his keys from his coffee table and his coat from the back of the couch. "Really. But he doesn't know about you."

"Seriously!"

"You want to pick his mouth, right? Best time to do that is at dinner."

Alex didn't have time to even look at Frank's couch before Henry arrived outside.

When he saw Alex step out with Frank, his brows furrowed.

"Alex?" He asked. "What are you doing here?"

Alex opened her mouth to answer, but Frank beat him to it.

"She's coming with us to dinner. Hope you don't mind." Frank said as he pocketed his keys and slid his arms into his coat.

Frank climbed into the passenger seat of Henry's truck while Alex took a seat in the back. She was starting to become too familiar with the truck.

"Don't mind at all." Henry checked his watch. "Shit." He muttered. "Sorry about this. I'm running late to pick up Juno. That's her." He said to Alex. He nodded to a picture stuck to the dashboard. It was a picture of him and a young girl, with his dark hair and his shrewd eyes.

"Sure. Wouldn't want to keep her waiting."

They drove on in silence. Alex expected him to ask her questions since he had mentioned having some of his own. But neither he nor Frank said a word.

She waited but became preoccupied with the sights of the buildings, cars and lights passing by. Henry seemed to be content with the silence. He didn't speak again until they arrived in front of a wrought iron gate that blocked the entrance to the enormous building that housed the school.

The headlights of the truck illuminated the same small girl with dark hair and Henry's eyes from the photo she had seen earlier. Only this time she was in a school uniform with a blazer and tie, and she was scowling. Her expression only served to make her look even more like her father, as she stomped up to the truck.

Her eyes narrowed in on Alex, and some of the harshness faded as she walked around the truck and climbed into the backseat, shoving her father's things aside.

"Hey, kid," Henry grumbled.

"Hey, Dad. Hey Uncle Frank." The girl muttered back. She slumped into the seat and dropped her bag on top of the pile of mess next to her. Her eyes blinked slowly, and she yawned loudly before her eyes focused on Alex. "Who is this?"

"Her name's Alex," Frank said cheerfully. "She works with me. Your dad found her at a bus stop." He said conversationally.

"Oh, hey." Juno yawned, waving at Alex. "I'm Juno."

"I said she could join us for dinner."

"Ok," Juno mumbled sleepily, as she pulled at her tie.

Henry navigated the truck away from the school and began to drive back the way they had come.

"Dad," Juno groaned, as a sharp turn around a corner caused the mountain of mess to topple towards her, "you can't just throw your stuff in the back." She nudged the pile of papers away from her, but they kept sliding back.

"Oh, really? So why do you do it then?"

Juno squeaked indignantly. "I didn't dump anything!"

"So where's all this come from?"

Juno poked the large flask that was peeking out from underneath the fast-food paper bags. "You probably. It's your files. And you shouldn't snack between arrests, you know. Or eat so much junk food. Soon the bad guys are gonna be able to outrun you. You're gonna be sitting on the curb watching them run off."

Frank chuckled darkly. "Well, I guess that junk food saved my hide a few times, then."

Henry shook his head. "Sweetheart, we all eat from the same place, eating the same junk. If anything they'll be sitting on the curb with me."

"That might be true across the bridge but what about here? Jazzy says that her dad takes his new girlfriend to fancy restaurants all the time."

Henry scoffed. "Richie acts like he's people, but I saw him coming outta *Freddie's* with ketchup on his mouth."

Juno laughed. "You saw all that? Did ya have your binoculars with you too?"

"Damn right, I did."

Frank and Juno both laughed at that and even Alex had to smile. Juno's laughs dissolved into giggles, before she sat up, her eyes wide. "Hey, for dinner, can we get a burger at *Freddie's?*" Juno asked, poking her head between the seats.

"I thought you didn't like all the burgers we've been eating."

"I didn't say that. I just don't like the trash. Plus, I just think you should add some greens to your diet. Maybe a jog or two.

Henry chuckled. "I'll work on the greens, but I do enough running as it is. And as for the trash, stop leaving it around if it bothers you." He looked down at his watch and sighed. "Fine. Let's do it. You okay with that." He turned to Alex.

"I don't mind." Alex piped up, looking between father and daughter.

Juno's eyes shone. "Really?"

Alex nodded, fiddling with the straps of her bag.

"I don't mind either. Not that I was asked." Frank grumbled.

Juno pushed at his shoulder. "Of course, I was asking you too."

"Well, thank you. It's nice to be remembered."

Juno laughed and stretched in her seat, pushing her arms behind her head, her back arching as she yawned again. Loose strands had started to come out of her ponytail, and it was only getting messier."Anyway, Alex, where do you live?'

"*Cassandra's Palace.*"

Juno's eyebrows drew together and Henry shifted in his seat. He kept his eyes on the road but his attention was focused elsewhere.

"Really? I don't think we've seen you around there before." Juno said thoughtfully.

Alex turned her head away, trying to preoccupy herself with the window and the cars passing by. "Haven't been there long. Have you been there a lot?"

"Not really, but we haven't seen you around before." Juno craned her neck to look at Alex, then around at the seats beside her. After a few minutes of silence, Juno was the one to finally break it again. "So, what kind of burger do you want?"

Alex looked at her puzzled. "How...many kinds are there?"

"Doesn't really matter. It's all grease and salt anyway." Henry grumbled.

"I thought that's what you loved about it," Frank added.

Juno smirked at the jab, but Henry rolled his eyes.

Alex sat back in her seat as both Juno, Frank and Henry argued about the best burgers. They threw out good-natured insults whenever anyone suggested something the others hated, insisting that their choice was the right one.

The banter between a parent and child, or even between an uncle and niece was something that Alex had never experienced firsthand.

She could barely remember her parents and had never been close enough to someone else to see their relationship with their parents.

When she was in Oakland, she spent time with an elderly couple. Max and Pauline had treated her well. Pauline had been kind enough to give her a job. But that wasn't the same.

She had never known what it was like to be so close to someone else.

Alex stared out of the window as she listened to both father and daughter.

After a long and heated discussion about the best burger fillings, both Juno and Henry began to talk about Juno's day at school.

At some point during the ride, Alex had drifted off and fell into a light sleep, as Juno, Frank and Henry joked about their day. Soon the topic segued to animal attacks.

Juno told Henry and Frank the stories that her friends had told her during class, about the animal that was attacking people around Kenzo.

According to her friends, some kind of demon was responsible for the attacks. They all had theories and experiences with the thing. Some caught glimpses of shadows following them. Some swore they saw it maul someone.

But all of Juno's friends had conflicting opinions about the nature of the creature. Some thought it was a craft demon bear. Or perhaps a demon-wolf. Some even thought it could be a demon fox.

To Alex, the most concerning thing was how vivid their imaginations were.

Though, Alex was pretty sure that whatever it was that had been watching her wasn't an ordinary creature, like a wolf, bear or fox. It was too dexterous for that.

The thing in the woods hadn't looked like anything she'd ever seen, and Alex had seen a lot in her life. She would have preferred to forget if only to be able to sleep better at night.

Henry reassured Juno that as long as she kept to public areas and didn't go off alone, she wouldn't have anything to fear and that her friends should do the same.

Frank stared stonily out of the windshield. "And if they tell you to go with them out in the middle of nowhere, you make sure to tell them they can kick rocks."

"Uncle Frank-"

"I mean it!" He snapped. "Don't go following those idiots into danger just because you talk to 'em at school, you hear? It's not safe."

Alex had a feeling that would do very little to keep Juno's friends out of danger.

No one would take the idea of an animal attack seriously, and the idea that a large monster, not just an animal, was killing anyone seemed so strange and unbelievable, that she was sure that most people wouldn't listen.

The conversation followed her as she drifted off to sleep and she began dreaming about a never-ending forest. A patch of gnarled trees surrounded her wherever she went.

No matter how hard she tried to get away, she never moved far or fast enough.

Out of the corner of her eye, she saw a dark figure with bright yellow eyes and spindly, shadowy limbs, lurking in the middle of a dense cluster of dead trees.

Every time she tried to run, she ended up where she started, as the monster came closer and closer to her, until it could touch her.

She felt a hand clamp down on her shoulder and she jerked up in her seat.

Alex was back in Henry's truck, fully awake, staring ahead as they pulled into the parking lot of *Freddie's Grill* once again.

"Hey. Are you ok?" Juno asked softly, leaning towards Alex. Alex looked down and found that Juno's small hand was resting on her shoulder. "We're here."

Frank turned back to look at her. "Wakey-wakey, sleepyhead."

Henry cut the engine and turned to the two girls and his brother. "Ready?"

"Yeah," Alex muttered, picking up her bag and swinging a strap over one shoulder. Alex, Henry, Frank and Juno all unbuckled their seat belts and climbed out of the truck.

Alex looked up at the diner's sign and her mouth began to water. "So you like it here, too?"

Juno nodded, smiling. "It's the best."

Alex smirked. "I can tell from the backseat of your dad's truck."

Frank and Henry joined the two, towering above both of them, as they began walking up the pathway to the glass doors of *Freddie's*. "If you two don't wanna eat..." Frank started. "You can stay in the truck."

Before either Alex or Juno could protest, Alex's stomach grumbled. Frank raised an eyebrow. "I'll take that for a yes, shall I?"

Alex frowned at him as heat rushed to her cheeks, but Juno took her arm and began pulling her into *Freddie's*. Juno led them both to a booth in the far corner of the restaurant and sat down, pulling Alex down next to her, while Frank sat opposite.

Henry was already heading towards the counter to order their meal.

Juno took off her coat and settled in the corner before she turned to look at Alex. "Uncle Frank said you were at a bus stop?"

Alex nodded, staring at Henry's back as he paid for their meal. Her stomach made another impatient noise. "Yeah, just waiting for a bus that never came."

Juno hummed thoughtfully. "Yeah, it's because of the body that they found a few days ago. Another animal attack. They closed the road down, I think."

"Then, it's a good thing your dad came along."

"Yeah." Juno chewed her lip. "So, you're living in Troye? In that apartment block? *Cassandra's Palace*, right?"

Alex shrugged and tapped her hand on the table in front of her. "I guess so."

Juno continued to chew her lip. "I thought you would've heard about it in the newspaper."

"Juno," Frank warned.

Juno blushed in embarrassment. "Sorry."

Alex finally turned to look at the girl. "Why?"

"Because one of the people that got eaten lived there." She added before she glanced at Frank worriedly. He simply shook his head and surveyed the diner.

"I'm aware."

Juno nodded again and leaned in closer. "Do you have family there?"

Alex's eyes narrowed. "What?"

"Are you staying with family or something."

"No," Alex answered shortly. She frowned down at the girl next to her. She had the same dark, scruffy look her father did and the same shrewd eyes, but she couldn't have been older than twelve years old.

Juno smiled. "You can come visit us sometime, we live in Brighthall. We can visit you if you want. At least then you'll have two friends."

Alex's eyebrows rose in surprise. It suddenly dawned on Alex that Juno wasn't trying to prise answers out of her for some nefarious reason.

She was just a young child, just like Cecil. This is just what kids did, right? They gravitate towards people they liked.

Alex nodded her head. "That'd be nice."

Henry strolled back over to the booth holding two trays loaded with food. "Here ya go. Tuck in. So, what are you two talking about?"

Both girls and Frank looked up as Henry placed their trays down in front of them and dropped into the seat opposite.

"The dead person that used to live in my new apartment," Alex stated conversationally.

Henry's eyes widened and he cleared his throat awkwardly. "Yeah, one of the people that turned up dead was found a few weeks back." Henry's eyes drifted to Juno briefly, but her attention was solely on picking apart her burger and reorganising the fillings again.

He turned back to Alex. "The landlord is a dick, but there's not much we can do about that."

"You could hit him again." Juno offered, her eyes still on her burger. Frank chuckled darkly, and Henry shot him a look.

"Again?" Alex asked.

"Yeah." Juno sighed, as she replaced the bun on the burger and shrugged. "He said something and then Dad hit him." She turned to look at Henry for confirmation, but he just shrugged back.

"He deserved it. Anyway, forget about him."

As she ate, Alex was unsure when they would start 'picking his mouth'.

She understood that some circumstances weren't desirable and could, at times, be considered slightly immoral, but he was having a nice time with his family and she didn't want to break the spell.

Though this didn't stop Alex's mind from working.

She tried to humour the idea that it was a regular animal, to ignore the incident with Charlie. But even without it, things didn't make much sense.

Alex was no animal expert, but as a child, she was extremely fond of animals and was quite knowledgeable about them too from watching too many wildlife documentaries.

From what Alex had learnt watching them, there were animals around the world that were capable of killing a human, but many of those wouldn't go out of their way to attack or hunt humans, especially if there was easier prey around.

There might be a few animals in the area capable of attacking a human, but how many would do that unprovoked? How many would go out of their way and out of their den, or nest to attack a human? And how many of those would decide to repeat the process?

This wasn't the normal behaviour of animals. She couldn't be the only one to see that, could she? But if it was not an animal that was responsible for the deaths, then logically that would mean that a human was doing it. Or something that appeared to be human.

Or that could mimic them.

What or who was it?

How long has it been there?

Was it the same thing that had been watching her at the bus stop?

Probably.

Frank remained pensive the entire meal, only talking when Juno asked him something. Otherwise, he ate in silence.

Alex picked up her burger and inhaled the hot mouthwatering smell. Her stomach growled impatiently and she took a large bite. She had almost eaten half in less than four bites, barely chewing before she swallowed.

"Hey, slow down." Henry chuckled. Both he nor Juno had not yet taken a bite of their burgers.

Alex tried to heed his advice, but she couldn't.

Alex finished the burger in a few more bites and then began to attack the fries. In between, she took large gulps of the sugary, fizzy drink inside the cup. It tasted vaguely familiar but Alex wasn't sure what it was.

"Well, that was impressive," Juno said as Alex began licking her fingers.

Alex shrugged and continued. She was almost done with her food by the time Juno had taken her second bite.

They ate the rest of their meal quietly, before clearing their table and heading back to the truck.

It was only when *Cassandra's Palace* loomed in the distance, that Alex realised that neither she nor Frank had tried to force anything out of Henry. While she wasn't sure what Frank was thinking, Alex felt that Henry was under enough pressure as it was.

If looking for answers lightened the gloom over Kenzo and made it safer for everyone, then she would pry that baton from Henry's hands and look for answers herself.

CHAPTER 18

On the day of the big event, Alex set out for Belamour. She dressed as smartly as she could, all in black. Her clothes weren't fancy by any means, but she wouldn't stick out like she normally would.

Despite that, the grandness of the hall the organisers had booked, still made her look like a 'street-urchin', regardless. The hall was full of decorated tables with refreshments and scattered around the room were larger posters, identical to the flyers she had helped hand out. At the front was a stage with a brilliant spotlight.

There was a significant, bustling crowd of well-dressed people, already, with waiters darting between them with trays.

She craned her neck around the hall until she saw Nicolette James speaking to Nina and a tall, thin grey-haired man.

They were all dressed richly, in outfits that complemented each other. Nicolette wore a floor-length lilac dress, Nina wore a short plum-coloured dress, and the man wore a lilac tie with his grey suit. Considering the way they had coordinated, Alex felt it was safe to assume that the man was Nina's father.

Nicolette and the man were in the middle of a conversation, while Nina sulked into her glass of orange juice. When she looked up she saw Alex. She pursed her lips and stomped over to her. Like most people, Nina was already taller than Alex and with her high heels, she towered over her. Her parents, on seeing Alex, joined Nina.

Nina looked sullenly at Alex, "Hey," She muttered before she stalked away.

"Glad you could make it." Nicolette greeted her. "Alex, this is my husband, Marcus James."

He leaned forward and extended his hand. "Nice to meet you."

Alex forced a smile. "You too." She took his hand and shook.

"I'm glad you could make it." Nicolette beamed. "I thought you wouldn't be interested in something like this."

Alex looked around at the crowded room. There was a large poster by the stage with a photograph of Marcia. "I felt like I should...pay my respects."

Nicolette smiled again and she patted Alex on her arm. "Of course! And I want you to know that Marcia knew that she was a little bit much. We both regretted how things went, so please, feel welcome here, ok?"

"Of course."

"I hope you'll enjoy the party." Nicolette again said. With a dazzling smile, both Nicolette and Marcus sauntered away after Nina.

Alex spent most of her time bobbing through the crowd, wondering what it was she thought she would find.

There were long, elaborate, superficial speeches made by people pledging to a cause. She tried to make conversation with some of the other guests but she quickly grew bored pretending to be interested.

Alex had almost managed to fall asleep standing up at the back of the room. She had considered sneaking out of the building, through the front doors, before she heard Nicolette's name being announced. Nicolette James ascended the stage and began a heartfelt speech in honour of her beloved friend.

She looked out at the crowd as the spotlight shone a blinding white light on her.

"Today we are here for one of my dearest friends. Many people knew her but not as well as I did. She always pursued justice and now we need justice for her. The police are failing us and more needs to be done to secure the safety of the citizens of Kenzo. I have a great love for Belamour and to show my love, I will be donating $50,000 to two charities. I encourage you all to follow in my footsteps and band together to help our beautiful community. We will be splitting the proceeds between the local businesses of Belamour and a charity that helps those who are homeless. In memory of Marcia."

The crow clapped and cooed in admiration as Nicolette descended the stairs to join them.

As she did, at the back of the room, the crowd began to ripple, and slowly it parted.

Walking out from between the sea of people were Detectives Lovett and Li.

They spotted Alex as the crowd backed away to let them through, and David nodded to her in acknowledgement. "I guess we shouldn't bother to ask what you're doing here anymore, should we?" He asked.

In contrast to his usual demeanour, Detective Li looked just as sullen as Detective Lovett did.

Alex flushed. "Well, can I help you?"

The detectives exchanged a look. "Don't worry. We're not here for you. We're here to speak to Nicolette James."

As if summoned, she appeared, cutting through the crowd of people milling around them. "Here," Nicolette announced. "What is it?"

"We wanted to speak to you in private. Is there somewhere we can go?"

"Of course."

Nicolette led them out of the hall and to the left, taking them away from the chattering crowd. People watched as they went, already gossiping amongst themselves.

Alex followed Nicolette and the detectives as best as she could, to the edge of the hall.

When she caught sight of a waiter, she waved her hand to catch his attention. He walked over to her and bent down to listen to her request.

"Hey, where's the bathroom?"

He pointed to the door the detectives and Nicolette had just gone through. "Go straight down the hall to the end, on your left."

"Thank you."

She left the hall but once outside, she followed the direction taken by Nicolette and the detectives. She walked slowly and quietly down the hallway, listening to their voices as they walked ahead along the grand corridor. She would admire the building if she wasn't running the risk of getting lost by wandering away from the main hall.

She managed to keep her distance, to avoid being discovered.

They ducked into a room, and Alex crept outside the door to the room to hear them better. It sounded like the room they were in was quite large, and they were somewhere in the middle of it. She would have time to run, once they finished their conversation if she wasn't afraid to run.

"I suppose you've heard about the death of Charlie Hitchman." Henry's gruff voice asked.

"Yes, I have." Nicolette's voice replied.

"Forensics have found a patch of blood in his basement that didn't belong to him."

There was a weighted pause. "Why are you telling me this?"

"You're a friend of Marcia Rosen. This is about her daughter."

"What-What is it?"

"While it's not enough to assume anything has happened to her. We believe that this DNA belongs to Marie Rosen."

"What the fuck!"

Alex spun around to see Nina standing directly behind her. She stared wide-eyed at Alex in shock.

"I'm sorry I can't do this," she ran back the way they had come. Alex opened her mouth to respond, but Nina already made a good head start.

Alex followed her lead and ran back down the corridor as the footsteps and voices on the other side of the door got louder.

Ahead of her, Alex saw Nina duck into the bathroom and followed her.

She heard the rapid clicking of high heels further in front of her and followed the sound to the girls' bathroom. The sound of someone throwing up came from the other side of the door.

She pushed open the door slowly. Nina was doubled over and was retching into a toilet.

Alex stepped forward tentatively. "Hey. Should I call your parents?

Nina shook her head.

"Hey, what's wrong?" Alex asked her. Nina pulled away from her.

"I'll go if you want." She offered.

"No!" She wailed in between breaths. Please don't tell her anything."

"Fine." Alex agreed.

Nina leaned forwards and grabbed a handful of toilet paper. She blew her nose and stood up. She wiped her mouth with the back of her hand.

"This is a mess and it keeps getting bigger," She whispered almost to herself. "It was an accident." She turned her large brown eyes on Alex. "It was just an accident."

Alex was about to ask what she was talking about when Nicolette burst into the room. "Nina? Her eyes moved to Alex and then to Nina. She waved her over. "Nina, let's go, honey. You need to lie down."

When Nina gave no sign of moving, Nicolette walked over to her and grabbed her arm. "Sweetie-"

"No!" Nina pulled her arm away from her mother.

"Yes, you do, sweetie. Come on." She cooed, caressing her hair.

Alex slipped away from the bathroom as Nina cleaned herself up.

The news of Marie's blood found by Charlie had shocked Alex, but she wasn't sure what that meant.

Was he responsible for Marie's death?

But, Nina had said it was her fault.

How did that link to Charlie?

Alex walked back to the main area. She looked around the hall and saw Victor with what she assumed was his family. Next to him was Irene and four children, three boys and a girl.

Victor spotted her but then looked away, but Irene caught sight of Alex and waved. Alex waved back. She took a step forward and almost bumped into another man.

She jumped back in surprise. "Sorry!"

"No. I am." He stared at her, his eyes running over her. Alex felt uncomfortable like she was under a magnifying glass. He had dark hair and honey-colored eyes. His angular face looked familiar, but she could not place where she had seen him.

He looked over her shoulder at Victor.

Victor stared at the man next to Alex in shock. Out of the corner of her eye, Alex saw Nicolette and Nina.

Nina looked like she wanted to be sick again and broke away from her mother's grasp to rush out of the room.

Instead of following her, Nicolette walked over to the man next to Alex. "Er, Grant?" She inclined her head and the man followed her out of the room.

Now, Alex had a choice. She could talk to Nina and drag her secret out of her, or she could follow Nicolette and the man, to find out what they were talking about.

Alex decided that she didn't want to put Nina through more stress than she had been through during the evening, so once again, she slipped away from the crowd and followed Nicolette. She soon heard Grant's voice arguing with Nicolette.

"I haven't done anything."

Nicolette's voice scoffed in disbelief. "Are you kidding me? After everything you've done, how do you not get that?

"I helped you."

"I never asked you to do anything! Certainly not this. You did it for whatever twisted kick you get out of this!"

"You act like it was...calculated. It wasn't. Besides, I think this is more about your safety than my actions. You have a lot more to lose than I do. I could always start again, but you have created an empire for yourself that you seem fairly attached to. Your daughter is too fragile. She's been wandering up and down Kenzo-"

"Don't you dare talk about her! I don't even want you looking at her."

"Then stop me."

Just as Nicolette began to retaliate, Alex felt a hand tighten around her upper bicep and pull her away. She looked back and saw that Victor, despite his size, had snuck up on her.

"You need to keep out of this," Victor said as he dragged her away through the chattering crowd. He left her by the main door. She looked over her shoulder and saw the detectives re-enter the room.

Victor saw what she was looking at. "Just go home and keep your head down. For your own sake." He growled and pushed her out onto the street.

CHAPTER 19

After spending the rest of the bus ride home, mulling over what she had heard, she had thought of her next course of action.

Matt Brooks had been the first to go missing after Marie. If Marie was the key, then was Matt somehow connected to her? There had already been connections to Elise, Marcia, Marie and Charlie, but they had all had different fates. What was it that connected them? The only other person that had gone missing or been killed in the past year that had a link to the others was Matt Brooks, another real estate agent.

Alex decided there and then to investigate Matt's company. She had no idea how she was going to approach this, but she decided to wing it.

Alex shook off the rain from outside as she pushed open the door to the real estate place. It was empty apart from one woman behind a desk. When Alex entered, the woman looked up in surprise. She looked around before she jumped up to meet her.

The woman was tall and skinny, almost awkward in her tallness as she towered over Alex. She smiled behind her angular spectacles as she came to a stop in front of her. "Hello. How can I help?"

Alex brushed the back of her hand over her forehead, chasing away the water droplets that dripped down her scalp. She had debated what she should say when she got there, whether or not she should be honest in her approach, or fish for answers. She had gone back and forth on that as she walked to the building, through the rain, but even now she hadn't decided.

So she smiled and opened her mouth.

"I'm looking for a house." She offered, hesitantly. "A year ago, I spoke to a man named Matt Brooks. He said that I should ask for him directly if I decided to come back."

The woman's face fell with every word Alex spoke. She clasped her hands together as she averted her eyes. Her tongue snaked out of her mouth and wet her lips, as her eyes searched for answers on the floor.

"He's...He's not with us." She cleared her throat. "He, unfortunately, passed away. He died."

Alex nodded, waiting for her to elaborate, but unfortunately, she didn't. The woman blinked rapidly, her eyes racing behind her glasses. "I would be happy to help." She held a hand out towards her desk.

Alex waved her away. "What do you mean? What happened to him?"

The woman's mouth twitched to the side, but she kept her eyes from meeting Alex's. "It was an unfortunate incident with an animal. Can I...?"

"When did this happen?" Alex pressed on.

The woman inhaled sharply, closing her eyes in frustration. "Last January. It..."

"Where?"

Finally, the woman's eyes met Alex's and they narrowed at her challengingly. Alex straightened her spine, dropping all pretence. "Where did it happen?"

"The police already asked every question you can think of. If you are a reporter, you are about a year late. If you're just after gossip, you'll be able to find everything online, or in the newspaper." She turned to go back to her desk. "If that's everything, you can leave. I'm busy. The business is being dissolved."

The woman marched back to her desk and stacked the files on her desk. As Alex looked around, she could see that the interior was in the process of being re-hauled. There were boxes stacked at the back of the room, posters being taken down, and items being packed away.

"What happened?"

"After Matt's death, there weren't as many customers, and we're being crushed by the competition."

Alex's eyes brushed over the half-packed boxes. "Competition?"

"Another bigger real estate agency, with more money and a bigger presence. We could barely compete and after Matt....." She shrugged. "So if you need a real estate agent, you should go with Lighthouse.

"I'm sorry." Alex offered. "About everything."

The woman shook her head. "It's fine."

Alex turned to leave. "I'll leave you to it." She said and walked to the door. As she grasped the metal handle, Alex turned back suddenly. "I'm sorry, but I need to ask. Do you have any idea what happened? I mean, you personally? What do you think happened?"

"I'm sorry-"

"Please?" Alex chewed her bottom lip. "A friend of a friend died."

The woman's face fell in sympathy. "I'm sorry."

Alex nodded. "We found him...and we just...I don't know...we need to find out what happened. That was the first murder. The police would have-"

"Murder? That was an animal attack." Even as she said it, the woman looked unsure. Her eyes pulled away from Alex again. "It was an animal."

"Ok." Alex agreed. "But then that animal knows how to open doors and lock them again."

The woman fidgeted.

"If there is anything you remember..." Alex prodded.

"I just...he was just looking...just scouting out some area by the new Lighthouse resort."

"What lighthouse?"

The woman shook her head. "No. Nicolette James' company, Lighthouse. He was scoping things out." The woman's eyes widened. "Oh my god! Maybe, she set her thug on him. She probably wanted to get rid of the competition and hired someone to kill him and make it look like an animal attack. Oh God! And she's killing other people to cover it up. She's making it look like-"

Alex shook her head, holding out her hand to stop the woman's wild fantasies. "I didn't say that. We don't know if that's true."

"But you said-"

"I wanted to know if you saw anything else, not that I would know what that would mean."

The woman pursed her lips. "You're the one that suggested-"

Alex held up her hand again. "And I'm probably on the wrong track. You were right. I should leave it to the police."

Before the woman could ask, Alex rushed out of the building onto the damp street, before the woman could invent any more wild fantasies.

CHAPTER 20

The first death had been linked to Nicolette, and Alex didn't think it was a coincidence that Elise knew Nicolette, too.

Initially, Alex hadn't given much thought to the previous tenant but it seemed to be something she would be unable to avoid.

She needed someone to tell her more about Elise. The best place she could start would be to ask *Cassandra's Palace's* elusive landlord.

That would be where she would start but she would need to find him first. She walked downstairs and thought about what one of the residents had said before about his car. It had been in the parking lot and she knew when he had left because of it.

When Alex arrived back at *Cassandra's* she circled the building to the back of the complex where there was a sparse parking lot. There were barely any cars there and they were all silver.

She went inside and after knocking on Sully's door for more than 10 minutes, Alex was sure that he was nowhere around.

While this had deterred Angie and the other residents of *Cassandra's Palace*, Alex saw this as the perfect opportunity to find the information she wanted.

She knew that Sully wouldn't offer up information he hadn't done to the detectives, so he would be extremely unlikely to divulge his secrets to his newest tenant. But Alex didn't need him to say anything; she assumed his documents would show all she needed to know.

With a glance around she took out the metal lock pick and got to work on his office door.

It took a few tries since it had been a while since she had needed to utilise this skill but she got in all the same.

His office was quite small but tidy and organised. Most of the room was taken up by a large desk that stretched across the furthest wall from the door. Cabinets lined the walls.

She broke into the cabinet that had been marked a-d and searched through the files but found nothing on Elise.

She searched the entire office but couldn't find any information even regarding the other residents. His computer was locked and she had no idea what his password might be. She didn't know his birthday or anything about him outside of his name. Sighing she began rummaging around through his drawers. Sifting through a bunch of his letters she found one address from Nicolette James. After a bit more searching she found other letters of correspondence.

The door opened and in walked Sully whose eyes widened in surprise before they narrowed in indignation. "What are you doing in my office?"

Alex stood from the seat, raising the letters in her hands for him to see.

"I'm going to call the police."

"Good, while we're at it, why don't we call a meeting with the other residents and talk about security and all the other things that you failed to address the past few months? It's strange, you seem to have time for Nicolette James. I'm sure there's a law about negligence isn't there?"

"You broke into my office."

"Your door was open."

"No, it wasn't." he hissed.

"Well, you can't prove that. I just came to see my landlord and found that he's been taking money to rehouse the tenants from Wommack."

"There's nothing to tell. It's not a matter of police business."

"Maybe, maybe not. I'm not exactly an expert. But I don't think the other residents will be happy to know that you've been accepting money and not putting it into the building. But we don't have to call anyone. We can just talk."

Sully's jaw twitched. "What do you want?"

"I want to know about Elise Chambers."

"What is there to know? She's dead."

"I heard that she was a therapist. She was living in Belamour but somehow she has an apartment in Troye."

"She was one of the people that was moved from Wommack to Troye. She had a bad divorce and lost a lot of money. While she still worked in Belamour, she had to downsize, I guess."

"Is that why Nicolette is paying you money?"

Sully's jaw twitched again.

"Is she blackmailing you?" That didn't explain why he's been avoiding the repairs.

"If I were to put all the money into the *Palace*, I would also have to raise the rent. Nicolette made it clear that she wanted the rent to remain low, otherwise, any tentative agreement between us would be over."

"So, don't raise the rent."

Sully scoffed. "I would be putting more money into the apartment that I'm getting and if I were to fix them, the apartments would be worth far more than what I'm currently charging for rent. Unless you prefer to pay more. The security suggestions that Mrs Quinn asked for were ridiculously overpriced. Thanks to the influx of Wommack residents that Nicolette shoved onto me and her demand to keep the cost of the rent low, I can't afford it."

"So, you have seen Angie's letters, then?"

"It's pretty hard not to. Even if I were to balance the price with the changes, Nicolette has made it clear that competition of any kind would break our agreement. I'm not looking for a fight, especially one that I won't win. I have known her for many years and she is quick to use any situation to her advantage."

"Alright, I get that. If you can't beef up security, what about changing the locks? What about people's boilers and breakers? That's just basic things that people need. Nicolette doesn't have to know about any of that."

Sully looked apprehensive. "A lot of the basics are quite expensive."

Alex sighed. "What if I told you that I had something on her, something that might incriminate her?"

Sully raised a brow, intrigued. "I would tell you to be careful." He thought for a moment as his jaw worked. "And that, perhaps I might be able to look into some of the requests."

"Some?" She eyed him.

"Some. Not all. Only the pressing ones."

"Well, they all sounded 'pressing' to me," Alex mumbled. "But I guess it's a deal."

She turned to leave when he called out. "You haven't said what incriminating evidence you have for her."

Alex paused. "And you haven't gotten to work on those requests yet."

Silence. "Fine. But it better be worth it."

She turned to look at him. "Is murder worth it?"

His eyes widened. "Who?"

"The requests. Then we can talk." With that, she left his office.

As she walked out of his office and to the staircase, she wondered what she should do next.

She would have to talk to others who had known Elise. If she was a reputable therapist in Belamour, then she would just have to research her online.

An hour later, after a quick lunch and brainstorming about her next move, Alex walked down to the library and searched for Elise's name.

After a few days of searching, she had found all of the relevant information about the woman including her untimely death. Sadly, it was no more detailed than what she had been told.

She also found the address of her business where she had performed therapy sessions.

Alex knew she wouldn't be able to find information about the patients that Elise had worked with, but she could find someone that knew her well. She had been Nina's therapist. Nina knew something, but Alex wasn't sure what that had to do with the monster.

After scrapping every plan she had for how to get information about Elise, she concluded that this angle was a waste of time.

KENZO

Everyone knew what had happened to her and had probably already asked and answered every question about it.

The best people to talk to were likely Spencer, Angie, Goldie or Sully.

But would they talk?

She thought back through everything she knew about the woman and her mind landed on Cecil.

The old lady had eaten her.

Was he right?

Alex used the rest of her time to discover more information about the other murders and even some of the disappearances but could find no link between the people, their ages and locations.

A few days later, Alex had become an expert in all the disappearances that had been happening over Kenzo for the past year.

The details of each investigation or disappearance had been confusing. Most of the victims didn't seem to have interacted with each other. The only connection she could find is that the ones who had died had all been found close to a body of water. Each of those locations had been connected to the river that ran through Kenzo.

The idea that it must be aquatic in nature, became more likely, but it spent a lot of time on land.

But the information she had gathered had been generic facts that everyone already knew. She wouldn't have the authority to question more people. She had been lucky with her last 'interrogation'.

As she sat in the dark in her apartment, she concluded that the best thing to do would simply be to talk to Sully again.

They had already established a relationship. He knew more than he thought he did. She just needed to find the right question. She couldn't tell him her suspicions since he wouldn't believe her and he might accidentally omit clues.

She and Frank hadn't spoken to Rachel. They had completely missed her by going to have a meal with Henry and Juno. And Alex had done her best to hide from her whenever she could ever since.

Alex knew she didn't have much time before Rachel would show up again. But she wasn't her main concern.

Whatever she was up against was bold, adaptable and intelligent.

KENZO

If it knew she was looking for it, then it was only a matter of time before it would come after her.

CHAPTER 21

As she climbed the staircase to get to her apartment, Alex heard the sound of stampeding footsteps clattering above her head coming down to meet her.

When she looked up, she saw Cecil fly down the flight of stairs ahead of her. He stopped a few steps above her. His head snapped up, and he stared at Alex in shock.

His eyes were bloodshot with a stream of tears running down his face. He held his arm out in front of him, cradling it to his chest.

Goldie walked down the stairs behind him before she came to a step a few stairs above them.

Alex looked down at Cecil as he cried softly. "Cecil, what happened to you?"

Goldie tilted her head sympathetically. "He won't say. I just came back from work and found him like this."

Alex looked up at Goldie before she looked back down at the boy cowering in front of her. "Hey, do you-"

Before Alex could finish her sentence, the main doors to the complex opened. All three of them looked up to see Sully stalk into the building.

His scowl deepened once he spotted them, but continued on his way to his office. Alex looked around but she had no idea where Goldie had gone.

Alex turned back to Cecil. "Why don't you come stay with me for a bit? Just until your mother gets back home, okay?"

Cecil shook his head. "I don't want to bother you."

Alex held up the bag in her hands. "I bought you back some sweets. Your favourites. You know, the ones you always like to buy?"

Cecil looked unsure. "Really?"

"Yeah, why don't you go upstairs? I need to talk to Sully." She handed the bag of sweets to him.

He hesitated, but reluctantly took it, turned and climbed the stairs.

She walked down to Sully's office and knocked on the door.

"Come in." His voice called.

Curious, she opened the door. She had been ready to coax him into opening it to her, with a lure of information.

Sully looked up at her, visibly relaxed. "Back so soon?"

"I wanted to talk."

"If it's about the requests the tenants gave, then I have already started to work on some."

Alex blinked. "Really?"

"Really. I'm sure you'll find out soon."

"Thanks."

Sully shrugged. "I am the landlord, after all."

The words nudged at something she had stored in her mind. "Did Nicolette ever mention Elise specifically? I mean, when she moved in here?"

He thought for a bit. "She mentioned that a friend of hers was going through some rough times and that she was one of the people moving in."

"But was there a reason for her being here?"

Sully's brows creased. "Not that Nicolette ever said."

"What about Elise? How did she seem?"

"I hadn't seen much of her since she arrived, but she was quite stressed. I imagine a therapist's job would be."

Alex chewed her lip. "Was there ever a time where she mentioned why?"

Sully paused. "You think Nicolette killed her daughter's therapist?"

Alex pursed her lips. "Astute, aren't you?" Alex exhaled heavily. "She has to be connected. It would be impossible for her not to be."

Sully nodded thoughtfully. "I wouldn't put it past her to kill a person, but this isn't like her. It's too sloppy. And like you said there are too many connections. Marcia and Elise. Charlie worked for her."

She agreed with what he said, but considering that she knew it could shape-shift into others, perhaps Nicolette was not the priority.

However, it would have to learn about her, in order to carry on a conversation to convince the other person.

"True." She deflated with a sigh. What confused her most was that it attacked like an animal, but its targets had been picked like a human would.

Did that mean that it was planning its attacks? That there was a reason for it, at least one that made sense to the creature. How would she find something that could change its form?

Cecil had seen it. The lady who ate Elise.

"I have to go." She murmured. "I'll see you later" She turned to leave.

"Just watch out. People won't like you digging around. It puts a target on your back."

Alex gave him a grim smile. "Don't worry about me. I think I might have one already." Whatever had been following her had been doing so from the moment she arrived. It was only a matter of time before it stopped stalking and attacked.

CHAPTER 22

When Alex walked up the stairs to her floor, she found Cecil asleep on the floor outside of her apartment.

His coat cocooned him. He had placed his bag on the floor, at his side. His head rested on his knee. As she approached, his head snapped up. He blinked at her with unfocused eyes in panic, but after a few seconds, he relaxed almost instantly when he recognised her.

"Are you okay?" She whispered.

Cecil nodded his head, wiping the sleep from his eyes. He stood up, bringing his bag with him.

Alex gestured to her door. "If you're that tired, why not go to your bed and sleep?"

Cecil opened his mouth to speak, but nothing came out. "Cecil?"

He tried again. "I...I should probably go." That wasn't what she thought he would say.

"Are you sure? I can-"

"I'm really tired," He insisted. "I just wanted to see if you were okay."

She smiled. "I'm fine. What about you?"

His mouth twitched. "Yeah, I am...tired."

Alex didn't like his evasiveness. "You know, if you're scared, you can stay with me."

His brow furrowed. "I know."

"If you're sure then, okay, but you can still come down for lunch. I have more pizza."

Cecil's eyes brightened and he nodded. "Thanks." He said and walked upstairs.

Alex wondered if she should stop him. Cecil seemed very frightened before, and Alex wanted to talk to him about it, but if he didn't want to say anything, she couldn't force him.

She was just about to reach for the doorknob to go inside when she heard heavy footsteps thudding up towards her with the rattling of bracelets. She turned her head to see Goldie ascending the stairs.

Goldie stopped in her tracks. Today she had dressed for the cold weather, wearing a long-sleeved black shirt, black jeans and heavy-duty boots.

She held up her hands.

"Hi." She said.

"Hey," Alex answered back.

Goldie looked around uncomfortably. When she saw that they were alone, she gave Alex a cheesy grin. "So...I might have jumped to some...conclusions."

Alex unlocked her door. "Oh really? What would those be?" She crossed the threshold, and Goldie stomped after her.

"Ok. Well, even if you don't want to talk to me, I understand. I did want to talk about Cecil."

Alex dropped her bag and keys on her chair. What about him?"

Goldie closed the door behind her. "You've been spending time with him, right?"

Alex rolled her eyes. Was there anything Spencer didn't tell Goldie? "Yeah? And?"

"You know, Cecil is a...sensitive kid. He's got an overactive imagination and recently, I think he's been getting himself worked up. He's been seeing things."

"What's he been seeing?"

"Does it matter? It's not real."

"How do you know?"

"Look, I've only really ever seen him hanging around the complex. Well, no... I've seen him on the bus a few times, but the point is, I don't think he has any friends. I mean, friends his own age. He says he does, but they don't come over. I think that's what's wrong. He just had an overactive imagination."

Alex shook her head. "There's more to it."

"Is there? He thinks there are monsters running around."

A knock at the door interrupted Alex's reply. Alex crossed the floor to her door and yanked it open. She blinked at her guest.

Spencer stood on the other side of the door. Goldie held up her hands. "See, I'm actually apologising. I listened to you. I can admit when I'm wrong."

Alex folded her arms over her chest. "It wasn't the best apology I've ever heard," she muttered.

"I apologised!"

"You said you might have jumped to some conclusions."

"See! I said it."

"You thought I was a murderer!"

"I'm sorry!" Goldie wailed.

"And you say Cecil has an overactive imagination."

Spencer had been watching the exchange between the two with some confusion. "What are you talking about?"

"Cecil," Goldie answered. "Keeps talking about monsters."

Spencer chuckled. "There're many rational reasons for the things going on in Kenzo, most of which don't include the existence of...monsters. Regular criminals commit crimes every day, sometimes terrible ones. Some of those crimes even have copycats of them. It's just a conspiracy that they are all linked."

Alex would have believed his explanation if it weren't for the fact that she saw Frank's dead friend walking around. A regular animal might have been able to kill and get away if a human was using it. It might have been that the cops were incompetent and couldn't do their job, but what about Charlie? Nothing human could mimic a human so perfectly.

"If you say so." Alex offered.

Spencer raised his eyebrow. "Do you have another idea?" His eyes bored into hers. "Please, if you have some insight, tell us."

"No insight. Just musings."

Goldie bit at her nails. "What did you see the night you and Frank went to Frank's friend's place? What did you see?"

Alex shrugged. "A dead body. A very decayed body." She was unwilling to tell them more since it had been so hard to convince even Frank who had been there.

Goldie made a face. "Ew. Yeah, you said he had been dead for a while." She turned to Spencer. "How can you stand that?"

"What?"

"Dead bodies. I can just imagine the smell. Yuck!" She retched.

He shrugged. "I'm used to it."

"Oh! Er, better news." Goldie pointed at Alex. "What did you do to Sully?"

"What?"

"He mentioned that he spoke to you about some of our issues and, guess what? He's actually been fixing things. He's starting with the locks. What the hell did you do?"

Alex scoffed. "I didn't do anything. I just spoke to him. Some of the things Angie wanted weren't affordable without raising the rent, but I asked him to do his best."

"Really? That was all it took? No verbal abuse, no... favours?"

"No! Actually, I think it's because I wasn't verbally abusing him that he was more receptive." That and the fact that she had broken into his office and put him in a precarious position, though he hadn't seemed to hold that against her.

"Where's the boy now?" Spencer asked.

"Cecil?" Goldie asked, puzzled.

"Why?" Alex asked. She stared at him as if she had only just seen him. Spencer stood by the door, his hands by his side. Spencer was a tall man, but nowhere near as broad as Henry or Victor were. His coat was a few sizes too large.

"I want to see if he's okay."

"He's fine. He mentioned going to meet his mom at work. He just left."

"Really?" Goldie asked. "I swear I saw him earlier."

Alex shook her head. "You couldn't have."

Spencer glared at her. "Fine. I have to get to work anyway." He stepped out of her apartment and stormed away down the stairs.

Alex slammed the door shut behind him and locked it.

"Crabby. I know his job doesn't pay well enough for this kind of stress." She clapped her hands together. "Oh! I just remembered. Sully's getting someone to fix my heater." She pumped her fist. "Everyone's gonna love you. My boss, Duke, says that you get free drinks for a whole night.

Alex smiled absently. "Thanks." She was still unnerved about Spencer's behaviour. She thought of going to open the door and up to Cecil's apartment when there was another knock at the door.

She opened it again to Spencer's flushed face. He was dressed differently than he had been a few moments ago, wearing a short brown jacket over his white shirt. He was out of breath. "What happened?" He panted.

Alex and Goldie exchanged a look of confusion. "What are you talking about?

Spencer stared bewildered between the two of them. He pointed at Alex. "You called me at work. You said it was an emergency. It was about Cecil."

Goldie turned to Alex. "You did?"

"No! I didn't."

Spencer ruffled his hair in frustration, skewing his glasses. "Yes, you did!"

Goldie pointed at him. "*You* were just here with *us!*"

Spencer looked even more confused. "I just got here."

As they all stared at each other, Alex's stomach dropped. "Cecil," she whispered.

Just as she took a step forward, her apartment was engulfed in darkness, and cries of frustration could be heard throughout the building.

The power had gone out in *Cassandra's Palace*.

CHAPTER 23

In the dark, Alex felt around until she found her couch.

"Just when I was starting to like this place." Goldie's voice grumbled. "We were so close and then-" a snap cracked through the air, "gone." She chuckled, almost hysterically.

"What tripped it?" Spencer asked.

Alex grabbed her bag and found a flashlight and a pocket knife. She hid the knife from them in her pocket but turned on the flashlight. The beam of light broke through the darkness and illuminated the room.

"I have another flashlight in my apartment," Spencer announced.

"We have to go see Cecil." Alex insisted. She didn't like the timing of the blackout. She opened the door hesitantly, and as a group, they exited her apartment. Alex sniffed the air. The hallway smelled like fish, rotting fish that had been left out in the sun.

Goldie gagged. "Wow, that stinks."

"What is that?" Spencer asked, looking around for the source of the smell.

"It doesn't matter. We just need to be careful." Alex whispered.

"Yeah, we could break our necks on the stairs. That's if Spencer's doppelgänger doesn't kill us first." She joked, but the tremor in Goldie's voice told Alex that the statement was more of a genuine worry than a joke.

Spencer didn't comment on it, but he looked around warily before he unlocked his door and ducked into his apartment. "Light, please."

Alex angled her torch light into his apartment.

"Over here." He directed her. He pointed to the right. He opened a drawer, rummaged inside and pulled out two torches, a large heavy torch and a smaller one. He turned on the heavier torch. The light was ten times more powerful than Alex's. He handed Goldie the smaller one.

"Can...can we switch?" She whispered, eyeing the torch.

Above and below them, there was a commotion as the residents on each floor stuck their heads out of their apartments to find out what was going on.

"We need to-" Below them there was a loud bang, a scuffle, a groan and a woman's scream before another thud.

Alex gripped Goldie's arm. "Go upstairs and find Cecil. Make sure he's safe and make sure it's him!" she hissed.

Goldie opened her mouth like a goldfish. "What do you..." She started.

"Just do it!" She pushed Goldie towards the staircase heading up the stairs, while she went down the other set of stairs with Spencer behind her.

They almost bumped into Greg coming up to meet them. Their torchlights blinded him and she held up her hand against the light.

"Spencer?" He stuttered.

"Greg? What happened?"

He blinked. "It's Angie! When the lights went out... something big...just knocked right into us." He stepped back and pointed to the foyer. He led Spencer and Alex over to a dark mass on the floor.

Angela Quinn was sprawled on the floor, unconscious. a small trickle of blood ran down her temple.

Alex crouched to her side and checked for a pulse. After a second, she found one, it was faint but it was there.

"Is she alive?" Spencer asked. He looked around, shining his torch around the foyer.

"Yeah."

"Good." He crouched down next to her. "We need an ambulance and police. Go get Sully."

"Right." Alex rushed down the hall to Sully's office to find that the door had been broken in. His whole office had been wrecked. Inside Alex could see Sully lying on the floor. Alex pushed the remains of the door open slowly and stepped in. She checked all four corners of the office before she ran to him.

He was covered in blood and most of it seemed to be pooling by his neck and chest.

"Spencer! I need help." She yelled.

Alex attempted to stem the bleeding, by pushing down on the wound, but the pain woke him up.

Sully opened his eyes in pain and panic. He thrashed wildly, trying to get away from Alex, but that only caused more bleeding.

"It's okay." She soothed. "It's gone." She heard the thundering of feet as more people arrived in the foyer.

"You..you..." Sully wheezed. His eyes darted around the room. "I...don't understand. You..." As he grew tired, he stopped struggling and rested his head against the floor.

Sully may not have understood, but she did. It had taken her form to attack Sully.

"What the hell?"

Alex turned and saw Goldie in the doorway.

"What are you doing here? Where's Cecil?"

"He wouldn't let me in! I tried! I asked him questions to make sure, you know, but I think that panicked him even more."

Spencer joined them at the door. He looked down at a weak Sully. "What the fuck?"

"Help me!"

Spencer crossed the room and began examining him. Alex looked at Goldie. "Payphone, call the ambulance"

"Ok." She scurried away.

Alex turned back to Spencer. "I need to get to Cecil."

Spencer nodded. "Alex. These look a lot like the marks we found on the bodies. How the hell did it get in here? What is it?"

"I think it's a shapeshifter."

Spencer didn't argue. He didn't scoff. He looked, somewhat relieved as if this revelation vindicated him.

"Go. I've got him."

Alex nodded and rushed back out into the foyer. More people had gathered, but they parted to let her through.

Once she had reached the fifth floor, all she could hear was her heavy breathing. Her flashlight was getting dimmer by the second. She slowed, to check her surroundings, but the hallways were empty.

Everything was quiet.

She walked to Cecil's apartment door and knocked. "Cecil?" She called. She knocked on the door. I know you're scared, but we have to get out of the building. It's in here. Please. I believe you. what you said before, it can change its appearance."

She listened for movement inside the apartment, but this time, she heard scuffling in the dark, from the floor below. There was a hiss and squelching sound, followed by a low warning rumble.

She turned in the direction of the stairwell, but the light beam barely reached halfway down the hall.

She knocked on the door again. "Cecil! Please."

Slow, sticky steps echoed down the hall and Alex held her breath. Her breathing had gotten shallower. "Cecil." She whispered. She tapped the door again.

When she looked back down the hall. She froze. Buried in the dark of the stairwell were two yellow pinpricks of light at the end of the hall.

Time froze as she stared at it and it stared back. She heard another warning growl before it pelted down the hallway towards her. She threw her flashlight at its head and it connected with a thick, meaty sound.

"Cecil!" She screamed and pushed at the door. It gave way and she scrambled inside as the creature skidded past. Cecil tried to pull her away from the door, but she pushed him behind her and tried to close the door.

The creature pushed against the door, throwing its body violently against it. Cecil tried to help her push, but they were being pushed back.

"The couch. Can you move it?"

"Yeah." He pushed the couch to the door and Alex tried to keep from sliding against the floor as the creature banged harder.

When the couch was against the door, she pushed against it and Cecil handed her a large kitchen knife.

"What do we do?"

She took the knife. "I-"

With a harder thrust, the creature pushed the door open causing Alex and Cecil to fly backwards as it squeezed into the apartment.

In the dark, it was only a black slimy mass with lights on its head. The lights did nothing to illuminate the room and the only benefit was that Alex could see that it was looking at her.

The smell of rotting fish was stronger now. Its low growl was heavy and moist.

It launched itself at her from across the room. Under its heavy weight, Alex couldn't breathe. She struggled until she heard a metallic clang and the creature pulled back with a hiss. Alex took the knife and plunged it into its side. It gave a high-pitched shriek and slashed at her arm, as it rolled off her, thrashing in pain.

Alex scrambled off the floor and grabbed Cecil's free hand, sprinted out of the apartment, and back downstairs.

She didn't stop until they had crossed the foyer, past the other residents and exited *Cassandra's Palace*.

It was only when the fresh crisp air hit her face, did she stop running.

She looked down and saw Cecil staring back at the apartment building. It was only then that she realised he was holding a metal pot in his hand.

She started to laugh hysterically, and Cecil finally looked concerned.

"Are you ok?" He asked.

Alex shook her head. "No."

She let go of his hand and vomited by the side of the road.

CHAPTER 24

Cecil hovered by Alex's side while the paramedics checked her over. The other residents had come out of *Cassandra's Palace* huddled together and shaken. Spencer and Goldie hovered nearby, talking to the other residents, but kept an eye on Alex and Cecil.

Sully and Angela had been taken away on stretchers and a few others were either being tended to, or answering questions.

As the paramedic left them, Alex cradled her freshly patched arm. She looked over and saw Cecil's large eyes staring off to the side. She poked him. "Are you okay?"

He shrugged. "Are you?"

She nodded back. "I'm great." She smiled, but Cecil didn't return it.

"It's okay. We're safe."

"No, we're not! It lives there. It's just going to come back later."

"Cecil!" A woman yelled.

Cecil looked up, startled as an equally pale woman, with dark hair, wearing scrubs under her coat, pushed through the crowd of people to reach them. She ran to Cecil and held him tightly. Only Alex saw how he tensed in her grip. Lydia pulled back to look at Cecil.

"What happened?" She looked from Cecil to Alex, and back.

She tried to pull him to her again, but he resisted, leaning into Alex.

Alex squeezed his shoulder. "It's ok."

"What happened?"

Before either could answer, Henry and David, joined the three of them.

Henry looked at Alex. "How are you?"

"I'm fine."

"You well enough to talk to us at the station?"

Alex tensed. "Sure." She stood, but Cecil clung to her.

Alex prised him away from her and handed him to his mother. Again he tensed in his mother's arms and Alex understood. "She's not hurt," she said.

Cecil stared at her for a few seconds, before he understood what she meant. He looked at his mother and after coming to the same conclusion Alex had, let her take him away.

Alex walked with Henry and David and climbed into the back of Henry's truck.

As they drove away from the watching crowd, whispering to each other, she couldn't help but feel that she was being arrested.

Her hands were free and she had chosen to go with them, but she could feel a cage closing around her. She wanted to run.

That was the adrenaline that was coursing through her body. She scratched at her legs absently as she tried to calm her breathing, but she only felt bile rising in the back of her mouth.

She stared at the back of Henry's head and for a moment she contemplated hitting him there. If she put all her weight into it.

"Are you ok?" Henry met her eyes in the rear-view mirror.

"Yeah. Just feel a bit sick. I think that was just the blow to my head."

"We will be there soon," David reassured her.

Ten minutes later, they were pulling up to *Kenzo's Police Department*. Henry and David stepped out and opened the door for her. She stepped out onto the pavement, rubbing at her arms from the cold.

She walked in with each detective on either side. The police department was quite small and only had a few people milling around.

Alex didn't hear the exchange between the detectives and the people there. She only noticed when they guided her into an interrogation room.

"Before you get the wrong idea," Henry began. We don't think this has anything to do with you.

"Or anything else," David added.

"Then, why am I here?"

Henry folded his arms over his chest. "We want to know what happened."

Alex took a deep, steadying breath and it was as if a dam had been broken. "We were attacked by a monster. A shapeshifter. It's what's been killing people in Kenzo, and Nicolette James has something to do with it. I don't think it's her, but she knows what it's doing. It killed Charlie and was pretending to be him. Today it pretended to be me, and Spencer."

There was silence while the two men exchanged looks between them. Alex wished she knew what they were thinking, but she had no clue. Even she wouldn't have believed herself.

"Why was it at *Cassandra's?*" David asked.

"I think it lives there. Sometimes at least. It was going after Cecil. I think because he saw it, I don't know. But it's been here for a while. And it's definitely not a bear."

Alex swallowed and licked her dry lips, feeling that she just made things more confusing.

"It attacked Sully. He had a secret deal with her, one victim was her rival and one victim was her daughter's therapist. Grant, her business partner. He showed up at that event."

She stopped for breath and looked at Henry then at David. "You don't believe me, do you?"

"You'd be surprised how much we do believe," David muttered. "We spoke to Spencer. He said what happened before the blackout."

Alex didn't know what to say. She honestly thought she would have to try and convince them. She felt a bit unsure of how to approach now.

There was a knock on the door. David opened it and had a whispered conversation with someone before he closed the door again.

"Frank's here to get you."

"You called him?"

David nodded, "We figured that would be the best person to take you home."

Alex looked between the two men. "So you believe me?"

Henry looked at her with tired eyes. "I think after everything we've seen. We have to."

"You don't think it's a bear or something?"

David shoved his arms in his pockets. "Bears couldn't get around like that. To be honest, a lot of the deaths in the past year were just marked off as animal attacks because the circumstances were too...strange. We've seen some things that don't add up. Bear was..the best explanation we could give."

Henry dragged a hand down his face. "If anything, this being a...shapeshifter makes some sense. As crazy as it sounds."

Alex sat back in her seat, she didn't know if it was relief or a cousin to it.

KENZO

As she stared between the two of them, it dawned on her that if two seasoned detectives didn't know where to start or how to explain what was going in, then this wasn't going to be solved in a way that respected the laws of Kenzo.

The creature needed to be stopped.

They would have to kill it.

That was fine with Alex.

But how would they begin to explain this to the public? There would be questions for them about the animal. Where they found it, what it was, why they hadn't found it sooner. The residents of Kenzo would demand answers and Alex was pretty sure they wouldn't be able to answer any of them.

CHAPTER 25

After letting Frank into the interrogation room, Henry and David began to clue Frank in on what had been going on in Kenzo for the past year.

He hadn't taken the information well. He was furious that Henry hadn't told him anything, for his sake and for Juno's.

According to Henry and David, Nicolette's newest building venture in Wommack had struck them as suspicious. Especially considering she had paid Sully to take in the stray tenants in the old blocks who couldn't afford other accommodations, including Elise.

"But why kill her?" Alex asked.

Henry shook his head. "It's why we keep going in circles. No matter what we come up with, there are loose ends."

"We did find something, however, in Wommack," David added.

"Like?" Frank drawled. He stood against the wall glaring at his brother.

Henry shrugged. "We didn't know what it was, really, but it might be a kind of nest."

Alex raised her eyebrows. "We should go there to find it while it's still injured." She stood from her seat and stumbled to the left.

David reached out a hand to steady her.

"I'm fine." She insisted.

David shook his head. "We're not going after that thing. Not tonight. You're not in a good state."

"Yeah, and Juno's home alone," Henry added. "Frank can't be in two places at once."

Frank narrowed his eyes, but didn't say another word. Reluctantly, Alex agreed and let Frank escort her out of the police station.

Frank had spent most of the car ride silent. Alex wanted to pick his brain but had fallen asleep before she had even asked him a single question.

It was the slam of the driver's door that had woken Alex from her sleep. She peered out of the truck window, to find that Frank had driven to his home.

"What are we doing here?" She yawned.

"I'm not taking you back to *The Palace* until we find that thing."

"I injured it."

"But it's alive. And we have no idea where the creature is now."

He stomped around his house and collected a bunch of pillows and blankets and dropped them on his couch.

"I can't believe that bastard never said anything." He hissed, as he tossed down another pillow to the pile on his couch.

"We didn't. Anyway, you wouldn't have believed him."

"I would!"

"You didn't believe in yourself. We need-"

"*You* need to sleep. We'll talk in the morning."

Though she wanted to protest, she felt faint. Staying up would do her no good, so she agreed. As soon as her head touched the pillow, she fell asleep.

When she woke up the next morning, it was to a plate of toast, an omelette and strong coffee.

As they ate, she went over everything she had found out over the past few days. Frank had remained silent all the way through breakfast. The only time he showed a flicker of open concern was when Alex mentioned Henry and David finding Marie's blood with Charlie.

"So, Nic's gotta be covering up something for her daughter. And she's working with this thing to cover it up. That Grant you saw, definitely wasn't him. Probably as dead as Charlie."

'Yeah, but it didn't sound like she wanted it to kill anyone. So what are its motives?"

"Food." Frank shrugged. "Maybe it wants her to owe it?"

"But why? It can shape-shift. What does it need her for?"

"I guess even a supernatural monster could do with a rich friend. Still, I think we should talk to Victor. If Nic's involved he'll know everything."

"Okay, then. Let's go."

Since home seemed like the safest bet to find Victor, Frank drove them straight to Duval. He barely bothered to slow down when they neared traffic lights, green, orange or red.

The ride hadn't done anything for Alex's nerves and she was glad to get out of the truck once they had arrived.

Frank knocked on the door without much fanfare and a few seconds later, Victor answered the door. Alex and Frank began scanning the room behind him. It was empty.

Victor's perpetual scowl deepened. His eyes moved from Frank, to Alex and back again. "What do you want?" He said to Frank.

"How do you know we want something?" Frank said airily.

Victor scowled. "Because you're never on this side of the river unless you're looking for me, so before I punch you in the throat, what are you doing here?"

"Charlie."

Victor's eyes narrowed. "Just hurry up and say what you have to say and get out."

"I think you know something about Charlie's death."

It was almost imperceptible, but Alex saw Victor's eyes narrow. He looked around the room before he grabbed Frank by the elbow and hurried him out of his house.

"Dad?" a girl called. "Just a minute, sweetheart." He called back over his shoulder. "I'll be there in a minute. Just give me a sec." He said as he ushered Frank away from his home and back to his truck.

Alex hurried behind them as Frank wrestled his way out of Victor's grasp.

Victor was considerably taller than Frank but at the moment Frank didn't seem in the mood to be restrained.

"We know you didn't actually have anything to do with it." She said quickly.

Victor and Frank both looked at her incredulously.

"Do we really?" Frank snapped. "Because, I thought, you know, seeing that the only person looking for Charlie was Victor and all of a sudden he ends up dead, that he might have something to do with it."

"There was another reason we drove down here looking for him." Alex shook her head. "I mean, I don't think he killed him, but I think you do know something, don't you?"

"Of course, he knows something! Of course, he knows! Charlie's been acting weird for ages and he's been with Victor. He's been getting him to do one of his little schemes. Oh, I'm sorry, they're not your schemes, are they? They're Nicolette's. I forgot you don't do anything for yourself. Not even think."

Victor's jaw flexed in irritation. "I don't have anything to do with your friend. I spoke to him, yeah, but he was working for Nicolette."

Victor shook his head. "Sorry about your friend, but I think you're grasping at straws here. I don't know anything and I don't think Nicolette does either. She was looking for him. She wanted me to talk to him."

"About what?"

"I don't know...something about construction and I guess." He checked his watch. "I'm sorry about your friend really but he just might have crossed the wrong person." He turned and walked back into his house.

Alex and Frank stared at the house in front of them. It was truly beautiful.

"I think he is telling the truth," Alex announced.

Frank scoffed. "He's not exactly going to come out and say that he got Charlie killed."

"The shapeshifter has been killing anyone it considers a liability. It might not have been Nicolette who ordered anything."

Alex looked back at Victor's home and marched over to the door and knocked again. He answered with less patience than he had the first time they knocked.

"If you don't want to tell us what happened, fine. But come with us to Wommack. We're meeting David and Henry."

Victor chuckled bitterly and went to close the door again.

Alex slammed her hand on the door, pushing it back open. "Seriously!" Alex snapped. "None of us can trust this thing. It's a *shapeshifter*. And it eats people. Most things don't negotiate with their food. We think its nest might be there. Whatever this is, it's not something you can handle. Please, just come with us and help us sort this out."

Victor scowled at her. For a long silent moment, Alex thought that he would say no. She was preparing to step away from his home when he finally answered.

"Fine."

Frank and Alex took Frank's truck, while Victor took his car. It took them just under twenty minutes before they entered the boundaries of Wommack. When they finally arrived in Wommack, they were greeted by Henry and David, as they stood by Henry's truck.

Henry glared at Victor. "What the hell are you doing here?" He demanded.

"I was invited."

Henry looked from Frank to Alex, to Victor. Alex nodded. "I thought we might need him."

Henry glared at Victor. "Fine."

They were out in the middle of a lush green forest, with only one long winding road to cut through it.

"Where is it.?"

David pointed to his right. "Keep going that way and you won't miss it."

"How long have you known about the nest?" Alex asked.

Henry's jaw worked. "A month." You didn't think to tell anybody?"

"And say what?" Henry growled. "It's not an animal nest. It...I don't know what it is."

Alex felt her temper flare. She could understand to some extent the secrecy, but if they were willing to fudge the details about the other deaths, killing this creature off-duty, should have been an option.

"That long huh?" Frank snapped.

"How do you know it's still here?" Victor added. "It might have moved on somewhere else."

Henry looked him directly in the eye. "There is a fresh carcass nearby, always is. That's how we know that it comes back regularly."

"Then-" Victor was cut off by the ringing of his cell phone.

He answered it. "Yeah?" He listened for a moment. "No. Why?" His eyes moved to Frank and his entire demeanour shifted. "Irene?" He said. "Don't let him back in the house. Make sure you keep an eye on the kids. Just do it." He hung up and looked at Frank.

"Irene said that you just dropped by. She wanted to know if we got into a fight because you were holding your left side."

Frank and Alex exchanged a look. "I stabbed it in the side." She whispered.

"She said Frank wanted to know why I was talking to the police."

"How did it know that?" Frank asked.

"That's not important. When he left he said he was going to pick up Juno for Henry."

There was a stunned silence before both Henry and Frank rushed to their trucks. David followed Henry's lead and climbed in after him. Frank looked at Alex.

"Come on!"

Alex shook her head. "You go. I'll stay."

Frank hesitated. "Go!" She yelled.

Reluctantly, Frank climbed into his truck. Both his and Henry's trucks drove back down the road.

Victor turned to Alex. "I've got to get home."

"I know."

Victor frowned. "You're not staying here."

Alex nodded. "I'll be fine. I want to check something out."

"It's too dangerous, come on!"

"Please. Just trust me."

Victor still looked uncertain and frustrated. "I need to check on my own family!"

"I know! Go. It's nowhere near here, so we have some time. Please, go!"

Victor gritted his teeth. "Look. I'll be back. Stay here!"

Alex nodded. "Ok."

She watched him climb into his car and speed away. Once he was out of sight, she began to walk. The nest wasn't as difficult to find as she had feared. It had been camouflaged by trees and branches, but the nest looked closer to a cabin and just as well built as one.

There was no door and no one inside. There were dirty rags, bones and the overbearing smell of rotten fish again. She knew there was a nearby lake. Perhaps it was aquatic.

KENZO

The nest was large enough to stand in, and possibly do a cartwheel, but there was nowhere to hide. She took her bag from her back and pulled out her pocket knife.

It was injured and running out of places to hide, now that others knew its secret. So she sat down at the mouth of the nest and waited for the creature to come home.

CHAPTER 26

Alex waited in the hollowed-out nest until the sun had finally set, taking with it the warmth and safety of the day. She sat vigilant as she waited for the shapeshifter to return home. In one hand she held the knife in the other, a pile of dirt. Victor hadn't come back yet, or anyone else.

She sat tensely, waiting for the moment that thing would launch itself on her like it had the night before. Even now she could feel the weight of it.

She had not seen it, only felt the flexible muscle and the suffocating stench. She had almost gotten lost in the memory when she heard soft footsteps approaching. She tightened her grip.

She waited for an attack as the footsteps came closer and by the mouth of the nest appeared Cecil. He shuffled into the cave, clutching his side.

The only light that illuminated the room came from outside and with him at the threshold, his face was cast into shadow, but she could still see the surprise in his expression.

"Alex." He croaked, his face was paler than normal, and sweat soaked his skin. His hair was plastered to his head. His eyes were unfocused and hazy. Alex took an involuntary step towards him when she stopped. His coat was a few sizes too large.

Where he stood, he was almost bent over in half cradling his left side. He stared at her for a moment before he swallowed thickly. He took a step towards Alex but she halted his movements when she stretched her arm out in front of her. His eyes flickered to the knife in her hand. "Alex?"

"Nice try. But I think we both know who gave you that." She pointed at his side.

She thought it would try to argue, to trick her that he was the real Cecil. It didn't. A flicker of annoyance ran across his face, but he didn't protest. Instead, his eyes narrowed as they locked onto hers.

"I'm not your enemy." It said, "We don't need to fight."

"You attacked my apartment complex. And tried to kill my friends and me. If you're not an enemy, then what are you?"

Its eyes snapped to the weapon in her hand, before moving back to her face. It barely moved a muscle, only waiting coiled for action. Whether it was to attack or to run, neither she nor the thing knew. But they both knew it was waiting for an opportunity.

"I didn't want to kill you. It's just better to attack first."

Alex stayed rooted where she was. No matter the species, it was first and foremost an animal. All it really cared about was survival. Any sign of weakness and would take its chance.

"Is it?" She asked softly "The residents haven't done anything to you. They didn't even know that you were there. They think that you're just a regular animal that just wandered into town and got lucky a few times too many."

"You don't. The boy didn't."

Alex blinked and she felt her arm sag by the elbow. The creature's eyes flicked at the movement and she straightened it again before it could move an inch. "So, that's what that was about. He said you lived in the apartment."

"Sometimes." It drawled.

"And the other times?"

It stared at her.

Alex scoffed. "Thought you would have preferred to stay out of sight."

"I do."

"For the past year, there have been 'animal attacks' committed by an untraceable animal. Along with other random, unsolvable crimes. If you had more restraint, no one would have even known about you. You could have stayed undetected."

"I have been when it mattered."

Alex could feel her arm getting tired, but while she didn't want to give it an advantage, she didn't want to be the one to attack first. And not while it still looked like Cecil. As she thought of the real boy, something crossed her mind. "Cecil figured out what you were." She taunted.

"You didn't."

Alex's arm dipped, but she readjusted her knife. It watched warily but didn't move. "What do you mean?" She demanded.

"There were a few times we crossed paths. I don't believe you detected me then."

"If you're talking about the old lady, in the blue coat, I saw you. And when you were Spencer."

"I was talking about our last conversation before that."

Alex exhaled heavily. "What conversation?"

It smiled.

How many other times had she passed the creature standing in front of her with no idea?

She rolled her tired shoulders back and raised her head higher, as her body begged for rest. "You see, that's even more of a reason for me to consider you a threat." She reasoned.

Though it had barely moved, Cecil's face shifted. For a brief moment, the thought that it was melting passed through her mind, but that wasn't it. His features were.

They were sliding, almost imperceptibly, but the more she looked, the more she realised that was what he was doing. Cecil's nose no longer fit his boyish face and his mouth had widened. Its new height had been hidden by its slouch. It had been shifting before her eyes.

Her temper began to flare at the sheer audacity of the creature, but a tiny part of her was impressed at such a conniving attempt.

Despite the warning bells in her head, urging her to attack or to run, she carried on, as if she was blissfully unaware of the direction this situation was heading.

"If you hadn't been so...aggressive, we wouldn't be here now."

"Most of those kills were just food. Throughout Kenzo, I kept hearing people try to figure out why this was happening. What was the reason...the...motive. I was just hungry and they were there."

"Funny how your lunch almost always seems to consist of people who Nicolette James would rather not have around."

"The first time was an accident. It was shortly after I arrived. She was arguing with a man in the woods. She called him...Matt, I think. She didn't want him to tell anyone what he had heard exchanged between her and her daughter. I attacked him in front of her. She said nothing. She ran. But she stayed quiet. She even changed her construction plans to accommodate me."

"What were Nicolette and Nina talking about?"

"The girl named Marie. In the same area we met, the two men had buried a body there. It was buried before her argument with Nina. The girl likes to go there to cry. I assume that the body belonged to Marie."

"Nicolette didn't tell you?"

It shook its head. "But the body smelt like her mother. The one you argued with."

"Did you kill Marcia?"

After a long pause, it answered. "No."

Alex scoffed. "Really?"

"Why would I lie?"

"If it wasn't you, then who?"

It shrugged. "Does it matter? She's dead."

Alex's jaw clenched. She and everyone else had dismissed Marcia's concern for her daughter.

Marie had been *seen* walking around. Matt Brooks had been dead for more than a year. If the creature was telling the truth, then she had been dead a while before that.

And neither Nina nor Nicolette had said a word.

Nina had been withdrawn and clearly distraught since Alex had met her, but Nicolette had brushed the death of her best friend's daughter away.

With the help of two men...

"Was Charlie Hitchcock one of the men?" She asked.

"Yes."

"Did you kill him?"

"Yes." He wanted to tell the reporter. I heard them. I only did as she asked."

349

Alex was about to say something else when the creature shifted. Its face had been caught in shadow but as it turned, a faint ray of light drifted over the planes of its face, and Alex froze in panic.

Cecil's boyish face had melted into the rugged, weathered face of Henry Lovett. It hadn't finished shifting and the result was a distorted mess of both Henry's and Cecil's features.

But somewhere in the middle, was something inhuman and scaly, and just like that she was dragged back to the day she arrived in Kenzo and the fear she had felt staring into the dark at the unblinking eyes of the creature in front of her.

Despite what she knew of the creature, she had almost forgotten that no matter how well it mimicked being a human, it wasn't one.

It was an animal, who saw her, not as a potential ally, but as food.

The only reason it was humoring her was because it was injured. She knew from experience how strong it could be. How strong would it be in its morphed state?

She had been lucky before, and it was weaker now, but how quick was it? If she timed her attack wrong, the mistake could kill her.

"Where did you come from?" Alex whispered. "You couldn't have just hatched, just like that, so how did you get here?"

"How did you?"

Alex tensed. "I'm sorry. What?"

"You're not scared of me."

For the first time that night, Alex laughed, almost hysterically. "Says who?"

"Not as much as you should be. Most are confused and terrified when they understand. Not you. What I am doesn't surprise you."

Alex readjusted her grip on the knife. "It doesn't matter, does it?" She pointed at its wound. "Does that hurt?"

It tilted its head mockingly. "Yes." It hissed.

Alex relaxed her stance. "Good. Because if I can hurt you, then I guess I can kill you."

The creature straightened its neck, and the movement cast its face back into shadow.

Its silhouette rippled. It shrank down inside of the large coat as its hair grew, longer, wilder and curlier.

Alex only had a split second to react, before the creature launched itself on top of her, with so much force, it toppled her backwards. Her back hit the floor, knocking the air out of her and she gasped in pain as she struggled to keep hold of the knife.

A slight, familiar hand struck out and latched onto her right hand. It twisted it, turning the blade to her. Her left hand was still clenching around a handful of dirt. She threw it at the silhouette and it recoiled from her with a hiss.

Alex darted out of the way, but it lashed out and knocked the knife out of her hands.

She scrambled across the dirt ground to reach for the knife, but it dove on top of her, clamping its hands around her neck.

Alex wheezed at the loss of air. She could see only a blur of darkness in front of her. Once again, its form rippled and its weight increased, crushing her. The hands around her neck became colder and clammier. She plucked at them, but they didn't shift.

She thrashed underneath it as her vision became darker. The bones in her neck creaked under the weight and she thought of Charlie dead in his basement with a broken neck.

Alex threw her head forward violently, directly into the creature. It recoiled again and its hands loosened from around her neck.

With a gasp, she inhaled greedily and swung her fist into the side of the creature. It howled in pain and she jabbed again, earning another scream. Its scream was high and feminine and familiar.

Alex dove for the knife again and the creature latched onto her leg. She kicked it in the face and crawled forwards to clutch the handle of the knife.

Before it had time to recover, she turned over and propelled herself on top of the creature. She raised the knife and buried it into its chest.

It gasped in pain and stared at her with eyes she had only ever seen in a mirror. The creature gurgled and slumped backwards. Its head hit the ground with a thud and its dead eyes stared up at the ceiling of its home.

KENZO

Alex sat back on her heels, trying to calm her racing heart with every ragged breath she took. She stared at the body in front of her.

The little light that filtered into the lair had fallen onto the shapeshifter and she couldn't help but stare at the face in front of her.

She had seen it so many times, but never like this.

Its last act was to take the form of its killer.

CHAPTER 27

Alex sat crouched by the mouth of the lair, watching the body slumped over six feet in front of her. She had no idea how long she stayed where she was, with her double, but the sky was already darkening outside and she could barely make sense of the shapes in the cave directly in front of her.

A beam of light entered the cave, she heard the clatter of feet scrambling over the ground, coming right towards her.

Henry entered the cave first but came to an abrupt stop when he noticed the crumpled form of the shapeshifter. He stared at the body in front of him.

"That's not me."

Henry jumped and spun around in alarm. The beam of light from his torch crossed her face, almost blinding her. When the light moved, she saw that Henry was pointing his gun at her. His breathing was heavy. "Alex?" He asked.

"Sorry. I'm me." Alex held her palms out in surrender. In her right hand, she still held the knife but had it pointed down.

Henry had no reason to believe her, and Alex was glad at his hesitance. "Juno thinks if you keep eating Freddie's, you'll be sitting on the sidewalk watching the criminals run away."

"Okay." Henry angled his gun away from her as Victor entered the cave. He spotted the body first before he turned to look at Alex and then Henry. "What the hell happened?" He looked back at the body on the floor.

Alex shrugged tiredly and brandished her knife. "I killed it."

Victor grimaced. "How do we know you're you?"

"It's her," Henry muttered.

"You sure?"

"Might as well shoot me. Don't know how I'm gonna get out of this one." Alex stood and pointed at the body with the knife in her hand. There was black sludge oozing into a puddle around the body. It smelt like rotten fish. The same ooze coated the blade.

She held it up to her nose and sniffed.

The two men stared at her and turned back to the body.

A phone rang. Detective Lovett pulled out his phone from his coat pocket and answered it. "Yeah. Thank god." He looked at Alex. "Yeah, she's fine." His eyes moved down to the body. "We don't have to worry about it any more. Talk to you later."

He hung up. "Juno's fine. Never even saw Frank."

They all stared at the body in silence before Alex asked the question on everyone's mind. "What do we do? How do we explain this?"

"We don't." Henry rumbled. Both Victor and Alex looked at him. He put his hands on his hips. "The monster's dead. It can't hurt anyone."

"You think everyone's just gonna accept that? What about Rachel? She's not gonna give up her story, or Marcia or Marie's death."

"Nicolette's gonna want this quiet," Victor muttered. "If she wants to keep her daughter out of prison."

"But people saw..."

Henry turned to her. "Saw what? Someone attacked the complex and thanks to your heroism, people's lives were saved. That's what we will tell Rachel."

"But, if you don't find the person that did this, she's gonna keep targeting you and David."

"Let her."

"We could get Nicolette to advocate for more money to be put into the police department, and donate to Kenzo," Victor added. "Let that be the angle. It's just a bad neighbourhood that needs some help. Nicolette can keep her halo. Agree?"

He looked at Henry and then Alex for agreement. Alex nodded and grudgingly so did Henry.

"I'll grab the shovel," Victor muttered and left the cave.

Alex held up the knife. "What about this?"

Henry looked up and shook his head. "Take it home and clean it. It's not normal blood so there shouldn't be much risk there."

"Especially when the cops are helping me clear this up." She joked.

Henry flinched at her words.

"I'm sorry." She said, "I didn't-"

Henry waved her away. "It doesn't matter. Was never gonna win any awards for 'Cop of the Year', anyway. At least this nightmare is closing up." He dragged a hand over his face.

Alex hummed in agreement. She couldn't wait to get back home. And...

"Wait!" She said suddenly. "What about Sully?" He had thought she attacked him.

Henry lowered his hand from his face. "There's nothing to worry about. He remembers you helping him. He probably just panicked from the shock. I doubt he believes it was you who attacked him. Seemed worried about you. Most of your neighbours were worried about you."

"Really?"

"Yeah. Who knew tackling a shapeshifter would make you popular? Goldie and Angie were about ready to take our heads when they found out you were detained. Even Spencer was more clipped than usual. They didn't say?"

"I haven't spoken to any of them yet. I stayed with Frank."

Henry nodded, staring at the mess around them.

Alex hadn't thought that her neighbours thought highly of her.

Though she wouldn't admit it, something about knowing that they would defend her did make her feel warm inside.

She had come to Kenzo to blend in. To hide. She had thought the best way to do that would be to distance herself from others.

359

That hadn't worked well.

Though there were issues that they needed to deal with, those didn't worry Alex as much as the threat laying on the floor in front of her. She didn't know if that was a lack of sleep or adrenaline, but she felt that this was the best outcome.

The rest would sort itself out.

It always had before.

CHAPTER 28

As dawn crested over Kenzo, Alex and Victor trudged through the dense woodland and to the road where Victor had left his car. Over his shoulder, Victor carried the unmoving body of her doppelgänger. Her arms swayed slowly, and they reached towards the ground, moving with every step he took.

The three of them walked in silence.

Alex kept her eyes trained on the back of her own head, watching carefully for any movement. If it were still alive, it would have an immense amount of patience and discipline to play dead for so long.

Still, Alex remained vigilant.

Once they arrived at the road, Victor walked around to the back of his car with Alex trailing behind, the only sound apart from the whistling wind being the jingling of his keys in his hand. He opened the boot of the car and swung the body off his shoulder and tucked her into the trunk. There were two shovels already inside, and other tools that Alex didn't get a good look at. As he folded her limbs into the car, Alex took a look at her pale face.

She had seen her face many times, but never with her eyes closed or so pale. Strands of her curly hair covered her face and for a moment, she could imagine that it was someone else. But as her eyes moved to the hands that were so familiar, she couldn't pretend, so she pulled her eyes away, as Victor slammed the boot shut.

It had stolen her face, but she kept her home.

Its victory, if it could be called one, would be hollow.

They climbed into the slick black car, and as she buckled her seatbelt, she caught a glimpse of thick dark blood covering her t-shirt and her hands in the glinting sunlight. Her hands were shaking from the cold. The smell was stronger now that they were in the car, thick and rotting as if it had been decaying even before the shapeshifter had died.

"Don't worry about it," Victor muttered, taking off his coat and handing it to her. "I'll deal with the mess later."

Alex flexed her hands as the dry blood flaked off before she took the coat in her hands. "You sure?"

"I always do." Victor turned the key in the ignition and began the drive to Rossum, as Alex slipped his coat on.

The sky lightened quickly as they drove, and Alex grew worried that they would run into someone on the road, and they would know instantly what they had in the truck. But they kept going until Victor parked the car at the side of a road that looked the same as the others. Victor climbed out and moved to the back. Alex stepped out of the car and followed Victor around to the back of it, where he opened the trunk and lifted the body out. "Grab the shovels."

Alex obeyed and grabbed the handle of the shovels. She slammed the trunk shut and followed Victor as he carried the body further into the trees.

When they had walked out far enough away from the road, Victor placed the body on the ground and took a shovel from Alex.

"Come on. Let's do this quickly." He said as he took the shovel from Alex and began to dig. Alex took the other one and joined him.

She hadn't dug a grave in a while, but it wasn't something she needed much instruction for. Alex wasn't a tall person, so the hole wouldn't have to be that big, just deep, if they wanted it to remain a secret.

She only stopped digging, when Victor did. The sun was now up in the sky, but the trees kept them shielded.

Victor climbed out of the hole and walked to the body. He picked it up and walked to the edge of the hole, but Alex held her arms out for the body. After a second of hesitation, he handed it to her.

The body was heavy and limp, and she felt strangely protective of it. Strangely, it felt like a part of her. She knew what it truly was, but in her arms, she almost forgot what it had been and what it was capable of.

Is this how she looked? Small and pitiful? Innocent and harmless? She shook off the feeling and placed the body in the hole. It would be safe here.

All their secrets would be.

"Why do you work for her?" She asked quietly.

Victor sighed heavily as if he had been waiting for her to ask that question. He didn't ask her to elaborate. He knew what she meant.

"It's a job. I just do it. Besides Nicolette didn't kill anyone."

"Are you sure?"

Victor didn't answer.

Alex's eyes narrowed. "You knew that people were dying."

He turned to glare at her. "Yeah, I did. What else did you want me to do?"

Alex didn't answer him. She had killed the monster herself, but she had only done so because she felt like she had no choice.

If she had been given one, she couldn't be sure that she wouldn't have chosen to stay out of it.

If she had a family like Victor, a home...

Alex dusted off her hands and climbed out of the hole. Once she was out, Victor started filling in the hole, dropping the freshly dug dirt on top of the shapeshifter's body.

"What about Marie?"

"What about her?"

"No one knows she's dead."

"Marcia's dead. Her husband died a few years ago. Who's left to tell?"

"Rachel was going to talk to Charlie. He wanted to tell her what happened."

"You wanna tell her that Marie's best friend killed her in some drunken New Year's day accident?"

"Is that what happened, then?"

After a long pause, Victor nodded. "Marie and Nina had gone to a party. Nina drank too much, thought she was fine to drive and crashed the car. Called her mom. Her mom called me to bury the body and dump the car. I got Charlie to help me. Next thing I know, Nicolette tells me that Matt Brooks found out, but something killed him. Something that really took to the idea of helping Nicolette. She *didn't* ask it to kill. But Nina panicked and confided in her therapist."

"And the shapeshifter took it upon itself to kill Elise. She just didn't stop it. How fortunate."

Victor scoffed. "I think you of all people know how hard it would've been to take it down."

That was true. But, there was still something else puzzling her. "It said it didn't kill Marcia."

Victor frowned. "It must have."

"It told me it didn't."

Victor's mouth became a hard line. "Either way. It's not a good idea to involve Rachel. You think it's a good idea to air this stuff, that Marcia's best friend and her best friend's daughter covered it up? Because I guarantee you that won't end well. If she does believe she'll investigate harder. If she does, she'll go for Nicolette and Nina, and Nicolette will come for you."

"If it were your daughter, would you want her in a shallow grave?"

Victor frowned. "I'd want to fucking know, but this won't work out the way you want. she'll drag you down and the rest of us. She'll send that reporter to find out how you knew, and all this stuff will come pouring out." He sighed. "I get that you want to help her, but you're gonna have to get used to doing some stuff that doesn't fit your morals."

Alex scoffed. She really must look innocent and helpless if he thought of her like that.

"I'm okay with lying to Rachel. She's hungry for a story. I understand that."

But she should know where to turn her attention, shouldn't she? She was blaming everyone but the ones responsible. Alex just wanted to point her in the right direction, the rest she can figure out for herself.

Victor eyed her warily before he turned back to the hole. "You go back to the car. I got this."

"You sure?"

"Yeah, you've had a long day."

Alex nodded numbly and turned away and walked back the way they had come.

She walked through the woods, as she thought of her flat mattress back home.

Since she had arrived in Kenzo, it hadn't truly felt like hers. It felt temporary as if it could be snatched away from her at a moment's notice.

There was always an underlying fear that if she got too comfortable, then it would be taken away from her.

But now she felt safe.

She caught sight of the treeline and Victor's car on the side of the road and sped up.

When she reached the road, she realised where she was as she crossed the road to sit on the familiar rusty bench.

At the bus stop, there was a woman and her young son already sitting on the bench.

The woman watched her warily, but Alex smiled at her and the shy kid. She looked at the long stretch of road on either side of them and sighed, sniffing the crisp, clean air, even as her mind worked.

Kenzo was safe from the monster in the lair, but as Alex knew all too well, there were worse things in the world, and they did just as well at appearing as harmless as she and the shapeshifter had.

THE END